HER
LAST
FIRST
DATE

HER LAST FIRST DATE

JENNY PROCTOR

CHaPTer 1

Zoey Williamson hoisted the second of her two over-stuffed suitcases onto the bed, yanking at the zipper. Stupid thing always got stuck. When the suitcase finally fell open, Zoey sighed. The tiny closet in the tiny guest bedroom at the front of her grandmother's house was not going to accommodate all these clothes. She looked out the window and down the familiar driveway to the street, where half an hour before, she'd tipped and said goodbye to her Uber driver. When he'd pulled up to the house, nostalgia had overwhelmed Zoey and she'd nearly leaped from the car, but staring at her too-full suitcase, spilling jeans and dresses onto the bed, her exuberance faded. Nana's house held so many memories, most of them happy. It was the house her mother had grown up in, the house Zoey had visited as a child every Christmas and every July. Coming to visit this time should have felt like a happy homecoming. Instead, it felt like a manifestation of her failure.

Well. That wasn't entirely true. Zoey *was* happy to be visiting—scratch that—*living* with her grandmother. She'd been the obvious choice to move to L.A. while Nana recovered from her stroke. Her parents were in Illinois where her Dad was still working, and her Mom was busy being grandma to Zoey's niece and nephew while simultaneously functioning as primary caregiver to Zoey's *other* grandparents. Even though Zoey had to upend her life in Chicago and move halfway across the country, it was easier for her than anyone else.

Still, she could have done without her mother's parting shot. "Really, Zoey, you don't have anything tying you down. No family, not even a boyfriend."

Mom had at least softened the blow with an encouraging hug and the optimistic suggestion that she might "meet someone" while she was in California. Taking a three-month vacation from the industry you've fought to be a part of for years? Who cares? There are new men in California! All sacrifices are worth it!

"If this is one of your ploys to get me married, it isn't going to work," Zoey had told her mother, though even if she'd never admit it out loud, she wouldn't mind a little bit of casual California dating. Nothing serious, of course. Not unless she found someone who loved frigid, snow-filled winters like she did. Her mom might have been a California girl growing up, but Zoey was a Chicagoan through and through.

Even work had made it easy on Zoey; the station where she'd anchored the morning news for the past two years had recently gone belly-up, leaving her and all of her co-workers trying to find a new foothold in the competitive Chicago market. But rumors had been circulating for months that the evening news anchor on Channel 4—a bigger and better station—was getting ready to retire and so Zoey had opted to take her time in committing to something new. It was a long shot for Zoey to even dream of the job. She was too young. Too inexperienced. But there was also talk that the dying network news industry needed fresh faces to stay relevant, to connect with younger viewers. What was she if not a fresh face?

Still, sitting around Chicago doing nothing, waiting for a rumored retirement to happen so she could swoop in and claim the job had proven worse than Zoey had anticipated. In the end, she hadn't been all that hard to convince to take a little break in Los Angeles. It helped that her grandmother was quite possibly her favorite person on the planet.

Zoey glanced around the rest of the small room. The dresser in the corner might hold her pajamas and underwear, but her jeans, her shoes...they'd have to stay in the suitcase. Or maybe she could buy some sort of shelving unit to push into the bottom of the closet space? Shelving would definitely help.

Zoey's need for organization was important enough to override her ineptitude when it came to anything like home improvement. And IKEA wasn't that far away. She had a master's degree; she was smart enough to follow a set of IKEA instructions.

Zoey crossed the tiny hallway into her grandmother's living

room, where Nana sat in a recliner, her home health aide, Cassandra, sitting beside her. Cassandra had given Zoey quite the education when she'd first arrived, detailing all of the ways in which Zoey would need to watch out for Nana.

"Ms. Emily," Cassandra had said, "does not like that she has lost so much of her independence. She will try and do all kinds of things she isn't ready to do yet. She'll tell you she's ready to try walking on her own, when really, she needs to be working on holding a fork. You have to be firm with her." Cassandra had glanced at Nana then, who had rolled her eyes. "Whatever you do, don't leave her alone."

Not leaving Nana alone had sounded intimidating at first; Zoey had some savings, but she'd assumed she'd have to get a part-time job to help cover her personal expenses for the duration of her stay. How would that ever work out if she couldn't leave Nana's side? But after seeing Cassandra's schedule, it wasn't nearly so overwhelming. Cassandra would be around every day until five. It was only evenings and weekends that Zoey was the primary caregiver.

"Hey, Nana?" Zoey crouched in front of Nana's chair. "I'm going to run down to IKEA and pick up some shelves for my closest. Do you mind?"

Nana smiled. "Too many shoes?" Her words held a slight slur, and it took her longer to get them all out, but her eyes were bright and sharp, which went a long way to ease the pain Zoey felt in her chest whenever she thought too hard about Nana's stroke. They were lucky, the doctors had said. She would likely make a full recovery, regaining the abilities she had lost with time and intentional therapy. It could have been so much worse.

"You know me," Zoey said. "I shouldn't be gone long. Less than an hour."

"In and out of IKEA in less than an hour?" Cassandra said, raising her eyebrows. "That's straight crazy talk."

Nana smiled, the lines around her eyes deepening into wrinkles. She reached out and squeezed Zoey's hand. "No need. I thought of your shoes." Nana's words were slurred to the point of being garbled, Zoey only just making out what she said. Nana took a deep breath, her jaw set, before trying again. This time, her words came out a little clearer. "Harry will be here tomorrow to put up shelves."

"Harry?" Zoey asked. She hated how hard it was for Nana to communicate, though Cassandra had promised it would get better with every passing day.

"My handyman," Nana said.

"Oh." Nana had a handyman? "Well, I guess that's great then."

Nana raised her eyebrows suggestively. "I told you about Harry. Remember? You stick around when he comes." She glanced at Cassandra and smiled. "He's *very* handsome. Perfect for my Zoey. He doesn't have a fancy job, but he does honest work. That matters." She squeezed Zoey's hand one more time then dropped it, relaxing her head back onto her chair and closing her eyes.

Zoey thought back through the many conversations she'd

had with her grandmother in the past few months. They talked almost every Sunday; that was a lot of conversations. She'd often mentioned men of her acquaintance she thought Zoey should date; the divorced son of one friend, the grad student nephew of another. It's possible she'd also mentioned her handyman, though Zoey didn't have any specific memories.

It was possible Nana had just been talking to Mom about Harry the Handyman. Those two had endless conversations about Zoey's waning marriageability with each passing year. Nana wasn't as vocal about it to Zoey, but only because she was more tactful, not because she worried any less.

If talking didn't require so much effort, Zoey was positive Nana would be reminding her now, detailing a long list of all the admirable qualities the handyman possessed, right down to his annual income and the presence or lack of a 401k. That's just the way Nana rolled. She never pestered people for the details of their lives, but they frequently volunteered the information on their own. Nana just got people. Understood them. She had this easy way about her that encouraged people to trust her, to let her into their lives in personal ways.

Which made Zoey suddenly worried. "Nana, did you say something about *me* to your handyman?"

Nana cracked open one eyeball, then shut it again, tilting her head to the side as if feigning sleep.

Cassandra chuckled. "I'd watch out if I were you. She'll have your first date planned before you can say IKEA."

The next morning, Zoey had almost forgotten the handyman

was coming to install shelves. Not so much that she hadn't taken a few extra minutes getting dressed, making sure her dark brown hair was a little more tamed than usual. She wasn't expecting much; she didn't know much about what constituted "very handsome" for Nana. The handyman could be balding and pushing forty. But just in case, she had at least wanted to feel good about her appearance. With her hair finally managed, she forgot all about it and tackled the rest of her to-do list.

Zoey pushed into her bedroom, a bag of toiletries in her hand, and yelped when she saw a man in her closet.

Her hand flew to her mouth, silencing her, but not before Harry the Handyman—because obviously it was the handyman and not some random stranger in her closet—jumped, knocking his head on one of the shelves he'd recently installed.

"I'm so sorry," Zoey said. "I forgot you were coming. I didn't expect—"

The man turned around and Zoey's words froze in her throat. She knew Harry the Handyman's face. *Everyone* knew his face. She closed her eyes for one heartbeat, then two, then turned and walked from the room, closing the door carefully behind her.

No.

It couldn't be.

Forcing a long breath in through her nose, then out through her mouth, Zoey opened her bedroom door one more time. The handyman faced her now, rubbing a blossoming goose egg on his forehead. He smiled when she met his gaze. "Hi?" he said, his voice a question. Why was his *Hi* a question?

Nope. Nope, nope, nope.

Zoey closed the door again, backtracking to the living room where Nana sat watching television. She perked up. "Did you meet Harry?"

Zoey sat down on the sofa, angling herself to face Nana instead of the TV. "Nana. Why is Harrison Beckford installing shelves in my bedroom?"

Her brow furrowed. "Who?"

"Harrison *freaking* Beckford."

"No, Zoey. Harry is installing shelves. *Harry.* The handyman."

"Your *handyman* is Harrison Beckford?"

She looked at Cassandra and shrugged. "I suppose he could be. He's always been Harry to me."

"Who is Harrison Beckford?" Cassandra asked.

How two women could live in the US, in *Southern California,* and not know who Harrison Beckford was, Zoey had no idea. His home renovation show was based in L.A., and it was all over cable television. The oldest seasons were free on Netflix. Home improvement stores were full of his brand. He had a line of tools, a line of home décor. He was literally everywhere.

And now he was in Zoey's closet.

Shaking her head, Zoey grabbed the remote from the coffee table and flipped to the home and garden channel that aired *Right-On Renovations.* She'd put money on reruns being on. Sure enough, it was only a matter of seconds before Harrison's face filled the screen, explaining the steps he was planning to take to rip yellowing subway tile out of someone's dated kitchen.

Nana scoffed. "That's not Harry."

Zoey looked to Cassandra for confirmation, but she only shrugged. "It is too Harry," Zoey said. "It's totally him. How did you even meet him, Nana?"

Nana shifted, peering at the television with squinted eyes. "He grew up around the block. He's been cutting my grass and doing odd jobs since he was fifteen."

Zoey froze. "*That* was Harrison Beckford? The gangly kid with the shaggy hair that always mowed your lawn?"

Nana smiled. "You remember him."

Cassandra laughed softly. "I thought he looked familiar. You just don't think you're seeing people from the TV when they walk in the back door all casual-like."

Zoey leaned back in her chair. "Have you never asked him about his work? The fact that he's a nationally known TV star has never come up?"

"Why would it come up? He's a handyman. *That's* his work," Nana said.

"Technically, she's right."

The three women turned to see Harrison standing in the living room entry, a sheepish expression on his face.

"Harry," Nana said. "What is all this nonsense about you being on TV? Is it true?"

Harrison moved across the small room and leaned over Nana,

placing a small kiss on her cheek. "I've got to pay the bills some-how, Ms. Emily. To be honest, I thought you knew."

The man was clearly at ease in Nana's presence, though of course he would be if he'd been helping her out since high school. He didn't look that old, but his show had been on the air at least five or six years. He had to be close to thirty.

He turned and looked at Zoey. "Sorry for startling you earlier."

"It's my fault," she said. "I knew you were coming over. I mean, I didn't know *you* were coming over. Just that someone, some not-famous someone, was coming." She swallowed. "Sorry. You probably hate it when people make a big deal out of it." She took another deep breath. She'd needed a lot of those lately. She stood up and smoothed her hands down the legs of her jeans before extending her hand. "I'm Zoey."

Harrison's handshake was firm and warm, and awareness stirred in Zoey's gut. He really *was* handsome. "My friends call me Harry."

"Harry, then." Was he holding her hand a beat longer than normal?

"Come on," he said, finally releasing her hand. It was *definitely* a longer than normal handshake. "Your closet is finished. Want to see it?"

Zoey smiled. "Lead the way."

She waited for Harry to leave the living room before glancing over her shoulder at Nana and Cassandra who both watched, matching grins on their faces. "Oh my gosh," Zoey mouthed silently, before following People magazine's "hottest home renovator to ever hit television" out of the room.

CHAPTER 2

HARRY WALKED TOWARD THE bedroom, glancing over his shoulder to make sure Zoey was following him. Zoey was . . . not what he had expected. Ms. Emily had shown him a photo of her big city news anchor granddaughter—some sort of promotional shot with her news team—and she'd looked professional and . . . stiff? Was that the right word? Or just, helmet-haired and blazered? She'd been attractive in the photo, sure, but she almost didn't seem like a real person.

This woman seemed so casual. So unaffected. She was beautiful, but not in that L.A. try-hard way, with the tall heels and hours' worth of makeup and teeny tiny dresses. With his semi-celebrity status, he got that a lot. So much trying. So many women that looked like they'd walked right out of a fashion magazine but didn't have a goal or a dream in their heads aside from looking great. He imagined his stereotyping probably did a disservice to the women he was so quick to categorize; he liked to believe everyone had a little bit of depth to them. But why did it feel like everyone was so afraid of showing it?

Dating was exhausting. Dating with his schedule in a city like L.A.? Pretty much impossible.

Harry stopped outside the tiny closet in Ms. Emily's front bedroom. He'd filled half of the bottom section with shelves that would accommodate shoes, jeans, whatever Zoey decided to stack. On the other half he'd installed a second hanging rack. He opened the doors fully and grabbed his level off the top shelf before backing out of the way.

"I know it's tough when you don't have a lot of space to work with, but hopefully the shelves will help," he said.

Zoey studied the closet. "This is perfect. Truly."

"Awesome." Harry turned behind him and gathered up a few more tools that he'd used in the installation and dropped them into his tool bag.

"I remember you cutting Nana's grass when I was a kid. I mean, not you, specifically. I just remember a skinny kid with a lot of hair. I'm assuming that was you? Have you really been helping out my grandma since then?" Zoey asked.

Harry hooked his thumbs over his jean pockets. "My hair was ridiculous in high school so I'm sure you're remembering me. I didn't come as much while I was in college, but yeah. Ms. Emily has always been good to me."

Zoey raised her eyebrows, a confused look on her face. "Really?"

Harry shrugged. "High school was—" He paused. He

couldn't really explain without getting too personal. "Let's just say that when things were tough, Ms. Emily kept me busy. She kept calling me, giving me random odd jobs to do around the house. It was stuff she didn't actually need. I repainted walls that were already painted, reinforced fences that didn't need reinforcing. But she knew I needed the work. Ultimately, all the things I did for her helped me decide what I wanted to do career-wise. Helping her out now is the least I can do."

Zoey sank back onto the bed. "How has no one ever covered this part of your history in a human-interest story? This is television gold."

Harry slung his tool bag onto his shoulder with a chuckle. "Ms. Emily warned me you work in the news."

Zoey immediately smiled. "I'm in between jobs right now so I promise your story is safe with me. Honestly, I'm not actually surprised about Nana's role in all this. Taking care of a teenage kid she thought needed some extra love sounds exactly like something she would do. But the fact that you're still around, that even with all you must have going on, you still come to her house to do something as random as installing shelves? It says a lot about your character. I mean, you could hire someone else to take care of her odd jobs. I'm sure you have the resources."

"That isn't what it's about though." Harry leaned against the wall and crossed his feet at the ankle, his arms folded across his chest. "If I hired someone else, or if she did, I wouldn't get to see her. Ms. Emily feels like family. Even when she doesn't have anything for me to do around the house, I still come and see her every couple of weeks."

Zoey shook her head, a baffled look on her face. "Are you even being for real right now?"

Harry cocked his head in question.

Zoey motioned to him with her hand. "You look like this. You do what you do. *And* you visit an elderly widow every couple of weeks? You cannot be for real."

Harry grinned. He liked flirty Zoey.

"I genuinely can't believe that Nana has been your friend all this time," she continued, "and her family never knew. That *she* never knew who you were before now."

"Actually, I'd argue the opposite. She knows exactly who I am. Which is why I love hanging out with her so much. I'm much happier as Harry, around friends, than I am as Harrison Beckford on television."

Zoey studied him for a long minute. "Fair enough."

"How long are you in town for?" Harry asked.

The light in Zoey's eyes dimmed. "A few months, I guess." She gave her head a little shake. "Sorry. I made that sound awful. I'm so happy to be here with Nana. She's one of the most important people in my life. I'm just still reeling from losing my job."

"In Chicago, right? You were a morning news anchor?"

Zoey's eyes widened, and Harry grinned.

"Sorry. Ms. Emily has been talking you up the past few weeks. Though, I admit, you aren't what I expected."

Zoey narrowed her eyes, a hint of a blush filling her cheeks.

"How so?"

Harry motioned to his head. "She showed me a picture. You were wearing this navy blazer and your hair—"

"No," Zoey said, cutting him off. "Was it a promotional photo? From Channel 11?"

Harry nodded. "That's the one."

Zoey groaned. "Oh, why, Nana? That photo was taken when I first got the job. I think I was trying to dress the part, maybe? Make myself look older? I swear that picture is going to haunt me to my grave. Is that seriously the only photo she showed you?"

Harry grinned. "Zoey, there are photos of you all over Ms. Emily's house. Plus, I googled you." He shrugged playfully. "Really I just wanted to tease you."

"I'm seriously at a disadvantage here," Zoey said good-naturedly. "How come I didn't get advance lead time to consult with Google?"

Harry frowned, but quickly wiped the expression from his face. Google hadn't always been good to him. The tabloids had been vicious in their coverage of his semi-recent divorce. "Maybe don't consult Google when it comes to me. Or, if you do, try not to believe everything you read."

For the second time since they'd started talking, Zoey studied him, *really* studied him, like she was weighing everything he said with careful consideration. Was it just that she was a journalist? Logically, that was probably it. But Harry's optimistic side hoped it might be because she was starting to like him a little bit.

"What else did she tell you about me?" Zoey finally asked, her gaze trained on him.

In truth, Zoey was almost all Ms. Emily had talked about the past few weeks. She'd been at a disadvantage, since her speech was still slow and had taken a lot more effort than usual. But she'd still managed to give her granddaughter a pretty glowing recommendation. "She said you hate olives," Harry said, his tone serious.

"She did? That's random."

"She didn't actually say that. But you look like a sane, reasonable person which means you *must* hate olives."

Zoey smiled. "Olives are revolting in all forms, especially on pizza," she said. "What did Nana *actually* tell you?"

"She told me you are as smart as you are beautiful. Which the olives obviously confirm. And that you like children."

"All true things," Zoey said with a grin.

"Did she tell you anything about me?" Harry asked, feeling bold.

Zoey chuckled. "I don't know if you want to know."

Harry raised an eyebrow.

"She told me I shouldn't hold it against you that you don't have a fancy job, that you do honest work and there's nothing wrong with working with your hands."

Harry laughed. "Wow. What an endorsement."

"Oh, she sang your praises, too. Said she was sure I would think you're perfect."

The fact that Ms. Emily had said so many nice things about him *without* knowing anything about his fame or his wealth made him happy. Zoey had clearly known who he was when they'd met, but he liked that she'd first learned of him, learned that her grandmother thought he was great, before she realized who he actually was. He never knew which way meeting new people was going to go these days. Half the people he met only wanted to ask him for renovation advice and talk about the possibility of being on his show. The other half generally cared a lot more about his money than they did his actual personality. Finding people that he could be real with? His celebrity made it tough.

But Zoey seemed pretty real. And she *was* beautiful. And her grandmother's recommendation said a lot about her character in Harry's mind. He imagined the words he might say if he were to ask her out. Was it too soon? Would it be too awkward? Would she be around long enough for it to even be worth it?

"So you're in between jobs now, I guess?"

Zoey nodded. "The station where I anchored the morning news went bankrupt and we all lost our jobs."

"Ouch. But there are other news stations in Chicago, right?"

"For sure, but it's a competitive industry. I'm doing my best to stay connected even though I'm gone for a few months. I'd love to do evening news somewhere—the schedule is so much better—but those jobs are even *more* competitive."

"I'm sure it's hard to step away, particularly when you could be networking, jobhunting."

"Oh, I'm still networking. And jobhunting. Every day. Maybe multiple times a day. I might not be in Chicago in person, but I'm trying to at least stay on top of what's happening at the biggest stations."

"Sounds like you're making quite a sacrifice to be here."

She quickly shook her head. "No. Nana's worth it. Besides, everyone else in the family *has* a job. The fact that I'm just looking for one makes me the obvious choice to be live-in caregiver. They've got jobs, pets, babies, obligations." She lifted her hands into a shrug. "I'm just me."

"Don't make light of it. You moved halfway across the country. I'm sure Ms. Emily appreciates you being here. How *is* she, anyway?" Harry asked. "It seems like her speech is a little better today."

"You probably know more than I do about that," Zoey said. "I only got here yesterday. Her spirits seem good, and Cassandra told me she's cooperating with her physical therapy, but she's not very good at resting. She hates relying on other people."

"Yeah, that sounds like her."

"Harry?" Ms. Emily's voice called out from the living room.

Harry smiled. "Speaking of." He held out his hand, motioning toward the doorway. "After you."

He followed Zoey back to the living room where Ms. Emily shooed Cassandra out of her chair and motioned for Harry to come sit beside her. When he lowered himself into the chair, she reached out and took his hand. "Have you found anyone to watch your children yet?"

Harry's eyes flew to Zoey. He usually didn't mention the kids until the end of the first date. Though, if she *did* Google him, she'd learn all about them anyway.

"Um, no. I'm still working on it. I've been taking them to my sister's house."

Ms. Emily raised her eyebrows. "Charlotte has four kids of her own. That's an awful lot to ask of her, isn't it?"

Harry's jaw tightened. Ms. Emily was right, something his sister reminded him of on a daily basis. But he couldn't just hire the first willing person with a driver's license to watch his kids. He'd been working with an agency, but the last two people they'd sent over hadn't worked out and he hesitated to risk it a third time. It's possible he was overthinking it, setting an unrealistic standard. But being a single dad was tough. He lived in constant fear that he was screwing his children up. "You sound like Charlotte," Harry finally said. "She's always reminding me how hard it is. I'm working on it though. I promise."

Ms. Emily looked across the room at Zoey. "While you work on it . . ." The *w's* in Ms. Emily's words were particularly slurred and she paused, closing her eyes and lifting a hand to her jaw, as if she could stabilize her speech from the outside. She opened her eyes, determination in her gaze. "Zoey could always pitch in and help out."

Suddenly Harry realized what was happening. Ms. Emily was too good to leave he and Zoey getting together to chance. She was going to shove them together.

"Nana, I can't—"

Ms. Emily cut off Zoey's words but continued to address Harry. "You only need someone to watch them during the day." Another swallow, another touch to her jaw. "And Zoey is experienced. She's been a nanny before."

Harry raised an eyebrow. *That* was useful information. But then, just because Zoey had been a nanny before didn't mean she'd want to be a nanny now. She had a career in something else. The nannying was likely something that had happened a long time ago.

Charlotte really would love a break from having two extra kids every day though. And Zoey *was* in between jobs.

"It was a part-time thing," Zoey said. "While I was in college. Afternoons after school, and then some during the summer. That hardly qualifies me. Besides, I'm only here temporarily."

Ms. Emily scoffed. "But that's all Harry needs, isn't it?" She looked at him, a question in her gaze. "Until you can find something more permanent? That would give Charlotte the break she deserves." She looked back at Zoey. "You said yourself you were going to need to look for something part-time. This is perfect. Harry needs a nanny. You need a job."

"When I said I thought I'd need to find a job, I was thinking of something more along the lines of fact-checking for one of the local news networks, or, I don't know, transcribing interviews. Things I could largely do while I'm here with you."

"Pssh," Ms. Emily said. "Why? Cassandra is here. I bet Harry would pay more than you'd get for fact-checking anyway."

The more Harry thought on the plan, the more he liked it. He trusted Emily as much as he trusted anyone in his own family. If she thought Zoey could do the job, he believed that she could. Plus, it wouldn't be the worst thing spending a little more time with her, would it?

"I could use the help," he said to Zoey. "At least until school starts up. And it wouldn't be full-time. We shoot early every day, so I'm normally home by four. Would you consider it?"

Zoey looked from him, then to Ms. Emily, then back to Harry. "I'll consider it. But I don't come cheap, Harrison Beckford. Let's go meet your kids. Then you can decide how much I'm worth."

Chapter 3

"RIGHT NOW?" HARRY ASKED, hope lighting his eyes.

Zoey shrugged. "Cassandra will be here another few hours. Why not?"

Harry ran a hand through his hair. "Yeah. That would be great, actually. I can show you around the house, run you through the kids' basic schedule. Then you can decide from there if you think it's something that will work for you."

"I'll grab my bag." Zoey retrieved her purse from her bedroom, noting Nana's satisfied grin as she passed back through the living room. She'd expected Nana to have opinions about her love life, or lack thereof, but she hadn't expected her to actually meddle. This was meddling at its finest. And yet, part-time nannying didn't sound like such a bad gig. She did like being around kids, and she imagined Harry would pay her more than a decent wage. Plus, it might mean getting to see more of Harry himself, which, even just for the view, Zoey wouldn't mind.

Zoey leaned over and kissed Nana on the cheek. "How long have you been planning this, you sneak?" she whispered, her tone teasing. Harry was nowhere in sight.

Nana smirked. "I have no idea what you're talking about."

Zoey rolled her eyes and stood up, pausing when Nana caught her hand. "Give him a chance, Zoey," she said haltingly. Zoey thought there was more she wanted to say, but she only squeezed her hand before closing her eyes and leaning her head back against her chair.

Zoey said goodbye to Cassandra, reminding her that she was only a quick call away, and then went to find Harry.

He was waiting for her in the entryway.

"How old are your kids?" Zoey asked as she approached.

"Hannah is five—she's the oldest—and Oliver is three. They both start school next month; Hannah will be in kindergarten and Oliver will start preschool at the same time. Their schedule will change then, but for now, things are pretty low key."

Zoey had all kinds of questions running through her mind. Harry was single; Nana never would have insinuated that the two of them should date if he wasn't. So that made him . . . divorced? Widowed, maybe? The thought made her stomach lurch. Maybe he'd never been married, he was just a really responsible co-parent?

A vague memory surfaced in Zoey's mind—headlines she'd read from the tabloids in grocery checkout lines a while back. It was a divorce; she was almost positive. Was his ex still around? So far, he'd made no mention of a mom being present in his kids' lives, no mention of a need to coordinate with anyone else's schedule. It sounded a lot more like he was handling parenthood on his own. Her heart went out to the guy. No matter the circumstances that landed him there, that couldn't be easy.

Zoey glanced at her watch. "I'll have to be back by five o'clock. Is three hours enough time?"

Harry nodded and opened the front door, holding it open for her. "My sister only lives a few minutes away and my place is around the block from that."

Zoey paused in Nana's driveway, watching as Harry loaded his tools into his truck. It was parked on the street, directly in front of Nana's house. How had Zoey missed it when she'd come home from the store in the first place? "Hey, I can grab Nana's keys and follow you over if that would be easier," she said. "That way you won't have to bring me back home."

Harry shook his head. "Don't worry about it. Honestly. It's less than ten minutes. We can talk about the kids on the way over."

Something fluttered in Zoey's gut at the thought of sharing the cab of Harry's truck with him. *Don't be weird. Just don't be weird.*

"Okay." She moved to the passenger side door and climbed in. The truck was enormous, the cab clean and roomy, with a full bench seat in the back. Two car seats took up either side of the backseat and a collection of stuffed animals and books, as well as a discarded hoodie and one random shoe filled the floorboards and the space between the seats.

Harry followed her gaze. "Sorry about the mess. The kids are always tossing things around in here."

"Don't even worry about it," Zoey said. "I think it's great."

"So, um, Ms. Emily's pretty relentless, isn't she?" He combed his fingers through his dark hair. It was longish on top and kind of wavy, and when he pushed it over to the side, it curled, just slightly, onto his forehead.

Zoey squelched a laugh. "That's one word for it. I think she's made her mind up about what she wants. We're the pawns in her grand plan."

Harry shot her a sideways glance. "You're not going to hear me complain about it."

Oh wow. That was flirting. That was definitely flirting. Zoey cleared her throat and tossed him a knowing look. "So, the kids."

"Right. Yes. They're great. Really. I know I'm biased because I'm their dad, but they're just stellar humans. Stellar miniature, slightly sticky humans."

Zoey swallowed. "And their mom?"

Harry answered without hesitation. "Their mom isn't in the picture. She lives on the East Coast, so she won't be around at all."

Zoey's reporter brain started buzzing. So many questions hid inside those few short statements. Why did the kids' mom live on the East Coast? How long had she lived there? Did the kids ever see her? But none of that was Zoey's business—she briefly wondered if Google could tell her anything but searching for him suddenly felt like a rotten thing to do—so she swallowed her questions and nodded along as Harry talked about the kids and their generally easy schedule. No one could accuse this guy of overscheduling them. It seemed like they lived a pretty chill life.

"So the days I'm shooting, we generally wrap up around three or four every afternoon. I aim for getting home around four thirty at the latest, which should give you plenty of time to get back to Ms. Emily's before Cassandra leaves." Harry turned the truck off of the main road onto a street not that different from the one where Nana lived. The houses were maybe a touch larger, but it had the same general feel. Midcentury, eclectic homes, palm trees, sidewalks lined with succulents. "That is, if you decide you want to do it."

"And what time do you leave in the morning?" Zoey asked.

"Anytime between eight and nine, usually. I like to have breakfast with the kids before I go, so I try to keep my mornings flexible."

"Wow. That's amazing. It's nice that you have so much control over your schedule. I didn't know Hollywood was so forgiving."

Harry wrinkled his brows. "I don't know that I'd call it Hollywood. And it hasn't always been this good. The first few seasons, I filmed on the network's terms and it was brutal. We filmed all over the US; I was gone all the time. But then when Samantha left and I had the kids, things had to change. By then, the show was big enough, I was able to make demands and they listened." He shrugged. "It was either that, or I walked."

Zoey swallowed. The hottest home renovator to hit TV in decades was also a really good dad. And that was really, *really* sexy.

"I, um . . ." She forced out a breath. "That's really admirable."

They stopped in front of a light blue two-story house that looked more like it belonged on a New England coast than it did in the suburbs of Los Angeles. "Wow," Zoey said. "Great house."

"Charlotte's husband is from Maine. It was his one demand for agreeing to live in California. He got to build a house that looked like home, hence the Cape Cod style."

Zoey climbed out of the truck and pushed her hands into the back pockets of her jeans, following Harry up to the front door. "So Charlotte, she's great. Her kids—four boys—are total maniacs though, so I can't promise you won't get hit with a dart or a bean bag, or something else as soon as we walk in." He paused at the front door, his hand on the knob and gave Zoey a serious look. "Ready? All senses on high alert?"

Zoey suppressed a smile and tried to match his serious tone. "Ready."

As soon as the door opened, noise assaulted her ears. Some kind of a Nerf battle was definitely going on, foam bullets flying past her head in several directions. She ducked and lifted her hands to cover her face. Harry grabbed her hand. "See? I told you." He towed her toward the back of the house, ducking around the corner into the kitchen. "This is a no-fly zone," he said, still holding Zoey's hand. "We'll be safe in here."

Zoey glanced at their hands, then up to Harry's face. He smiled, squeezing her hand lightly before letting it go. Did that mean something? That little squeeze? Zoey felt completely upended.

"Daddy?"

Harry turned around and caught the little girl that came barreling across the room. He swept her up into his arms. "Hey, Hannah banana. How was your day?"

Hannah sighed with dramatic flair. "Horrible. The boys were ridiculous."

Harry tossed Zoey a quick glance over his shoulder, a smile in his eyes. "Ridiculous, huh? Where's Oliver?"

"In the bathtub. He got goop on him and Aunt Charlotte said it was so gross, he needed a bath."

"What kind of goop?"

Hannah shrugged. "The goopy kind?"

"Glue," a woman said as she came around the corner into the kitchen. It had to be Charlotte. She had Harry's matching eyes. "The *glue* kind of goop. An entire bottle of Elmer's spread on every inch of his body. You'd have been proud of how thorough he was."

"Wow," Harry said. "I owe you dinner, don't I?"

"You owe me way more than dinner, little brother. Way more."

Harry stepped out of the way and motioned to Zoey. "Speaking of, this is Zoey. She's Ms. Emily's granddaughter. She's thinking about helping out with the kids until school starts back."

Charlotte looked from Harry to Zoey and then back again. "Truly?" she said to Zoey.

Zoey lifted her shoulders and smiled. "Maybe? I mean, I'm just meeting the kids right now. Feeling things out. But . . . probably?"

Charlotte stepped forward and wrapped her arms around Zoey, squeezing her so tightly, Zoey couldn't even move to return the hug. "I was about to tease you about how much I know your grandma wants you and my brother to get together, but you've just made me so happy, I won't do it."

Charlotte finally released her but kept her hands on Zoey's arms. "I promise the glue thing doesn't happen every day. Ollie is really sweet. The sweetest."

As if on cue, a little boy who could only be Oliver came toddling into the kitchen, his arms outstretched. "Daddy!"

Zoey didn't even have time to process why Charlotte knew about her grandma's designs to get her and Harry together before Harry grabbed her attention, setting Hannah down and picking up his son, snuggling him against his chest. "Hey, little man. I hear you made a mess."

"I all clean," Oliver said.

Watching Harrison Beckford be a dad? Zoey was really going to like this job.

Harry turned toward her, wrapping his free arm around Hannah. "Hey, guys? I want you to meet Zoey. This is Ms.

Emily's granddaughter. She might be spending some time with you guys this summer."

Zoey reached over and touched Oliver's back. "Hi, Oliver." He smiled shyly then tucked his chin into his dad's shoulder.

Hannah looked up at Zoey with wide eyes. Oh, she was *so* going to be spending time with these kids this summer. One look and she was already a goner. She crouched down in front of Hannah. "It's nice to meet you, Hannah."

Hannah took a deep breath. "I like Ms. Emily a lot."

Zoey smiled. "Me too."

"Want to see my pony collection?"

Zoey nodded, happy to have been so readily accepted. "Absolutely, I do." She took Hannah's hand and followed her toward what she assumed was the living room. She glanced back over her shoulder and met Harry's gaze. His smile was warm, and there was a look of . . . *something* on his face that made her skin tingle and her heart squeeze. Maybe it was the kids and the way he interacted with them. Maybe it was his history with Nana. Maybe it was the way his eyes crinkled up when he smiled. But Zoey really, really liked this guy.

She'd be lying to herself if she pretended that the fact he was Harrison Beckford and not just Harry the Handyman didn't have something to do with her growing fascination. But she'd seen enough in the past hour that she was pretty sure she'd be equally as charmed even if he didn't have celebrity status. As long as he still had those same smile lines around those same smoky gray eyes.

They hung out at Charlotte's a few more minutes before loading up the kids and driving a handful of blocks to Harry's house. They pulled up to an automated gate and Zoey tried not to crane her neck to catch sight of the house. She'd naturally assumed that Harry had money, but she wouldn't peg him as a guy that needed the mansion to prove it. Sure enough, they pulled up the winding drive to a house that looked a lot more California than Charlotte's but wasn't much bigger in size. The house had two stories, but it still managed a low profile, as if it was nestled into the ground and the surrounding landscape. A huge front door and massive windows and clean modern lines that extended around the side of the house unified everything in a way that Zoey liked, even though she didn't understand why. The house just worked.

"It's gorgeous," she said as Harry stopped the car.

"Thanks. I built it myself."

"Oh, right. I guess that makes sense."

"We've only been in it six months," he said. "It was a labor of love that I started before Hannah was born."

"Wow. So you did it *all* by yourself? No help at all?" Zoey opened the back door and reached for Oliver's car seat buckles. "Hey, little man. You okay if I help you out of your seat?"

Oliver looked toward his dad, who gave him an encouraging nod, then nodded slowly at Zoey. He pushed his thumb into his mouth as she unsnapped him. She lifted him out and put him down on the ground where he promptly ran toward the front door.

"I had help with the framing," Harry said. "That's a tough one-man job, but otherwise, it was just me. It was my therapy, working on it alone. It got me through years of failed marriage therapy, through two kids, through a divorce. I think life makes more sense when you're working with your hands, you know?"

She nodded. She wasn't particularly handy herself, but she could still relate. She felt the same way about yoga. "What's your therapy now that the house is done?"

He smirked. "So *that's* why I'm feeling all out of sorts." He handed Hannah her backpack. "Don't forget to take this inside, Hannah."

The inside of the house was even better than the outside. It was an open-concept floor plan, with the living room flowing into the kitchen and dining area then back into a play area for the kids. It was warm and welcoming and even though it was magazine-level gorgeous, it still felt lived in, like she didn't need to worry about breaking a dish or scuffing the floor.

"This is amazing," Zoey said, taking it all in. "Truly."

Harry's face lit up in genuine surprise. "You think so?"

"Are you kidding? It's spectacular." Zoey walked toward the kitchen. "Has it been on your show?"

Harry shook his head. "Believe me, the producers have asked. But with the kids . . . I don't know. I wanted to have something that was just ours. I keep meaning to plan a dinner or something, invite some friends and family over to have a housewarming thing, but I've been busy, I guess. I haven't gotten around to it."

"I can't imagine how you juggle it all."

Oliver walked toward where they stood in the kitchen, a book in his hands, and surprised them both when he passed Harry and held the book out to Zoey. "Story?" he asked.

Zoey looked at Harry and he smiled. "I think he likes you."

She took the book. "I'd love to read you a story, Ollie."

"Hey, are you okay with dogs?" Harry called. "We've got one, and she's enormous. If I let her out, she's probably going to maul you."

"I love dogs," Zoey said. "Go for it." She reached the living room sofa where she pulled Oliver onto her lap and opened the book. Before she could start the first page, a massive curly-haired golden doodle came careening around the couch, nails clicking against the wood floors.

"Goldy!" Oliver yelled. The dog licked Oliver with a gentleness that surprised Zoey, then snuffled into her leg, tail wagging enthusiastically.

"Hi, Goldy," Zoey said. "You're adorable."

Harry reappeared, crossing to the back door. "Hey look, she didn't eat you."

"I think Ollie protected me," Zoey said.

"Ah, smart. She's always gentler with the kids. Marigold!" he called. "Come on, girl. Time to go out."

Zoey pulled Oliver a little closer, wondering for the millionth time how she wound up in Harrison Beckford's living room, snuggling with his kid, hearing stories about his dog, when she hadn't even known him two hours before.

She'd thought a lot about what returning to life in Southern California was going to feel like. She'd never thought it would be anything like this.

CHAPTER 4

SHE WAS TOO GOOD to be true.

She had to be.

She liked his kids.

His kids liked her.

She had a warm smile that she shared generously; she had this quiet, effortless confidence that he found sexy; she was chill and easy to be around; and so far, she'd only asked him one question about his show, which didn't count since it had actually been about his house.

He wanted to ask her out. He was *going* to ask her out. Except, when? The kids had already been at his sister's house all day. They couldn't go back there. His mom and stepdad were pretty good about coming over in the evenings, and Samantha's parents were always willing to keep the kids, but then, the whole point of Zoey being in California in the first place was so she could stay with Ms. Emily in the evenings and on the weekends.

Which meant . . . daytime dates? But during the day, he was working and now, hopefully, Zoey would be with his kids.

Dating-wise, their schedules would allow for . . . basically nothing. Bet Ms. Emily hadn't thought this part through.

Zoey crossed into the kitchen, her bag pulled onto her shoulder. "Why are you frowning?" she asked.

He almost told her; she knew as well as he did what her grandmother hoped for. But then he remembered the way she'd sidestepped the conversation when he'd brought it up as they left Ms. Emily's house earlier, and he chickened out. If he asked and she said no, would it make her want to turn down the job? He liked her, but he needed someone to help out with the kids more than he needed a date. "Um, nothing. Sorry. Thinking about a work thing."

"Oh. Okay, well, I have to be back by five, so if it's all right with you, I'm going to take off. It's close enough that I can walk home."

"You don't need to do that. I'll drive you. I need to pick up dinner for the kids anyway."

"Are you sure? I mapped it. It shouldn't take more than twenty minutes."

"Yeah, but it's July. Don't do that to yourself unless you have to."

Her shoulders dropped. "True."

"So, what do you think?" Harry asked, reaching for his keys. "Who's hungry?" he called into the living room. "Get your shoes on and we'll go get some dinner."

"What do I think?" Zoey asked.

"About the job?" Harry prompted.

"Oh! The job. Of course I want the job. Your kids are dolls."

Harry smiled. "They really are. Here." He pulled out his phone, unlocked it, then handed it to Zoey. "Do you mind giving me your number? I'll text you later and we can talk about pay and that sort of thing. Can you start on Monday?" Really, he could stand her starting tomorrow, but there was only one day left in the week and giving her the weekend to get settled at Emily's felt like the right thing to do.

Zoey nodded. "Sure."

The look on her face told Harry she had something she wanted to say, but maybe wasn't sure how to say it.

"What?" he asked. "You can ask me anything. I don't want to pressure you into saying yes if you have hesitations."

"No, no, it's not that." She glanced around the room. "But I do want to ask . . ." She shook her head. "It's not my business, but I guess I want to understand what happened." She looked over her shoulder toward the living room where Hannah was helping Oliver put on his shoes. "Will they talk about their mom? Ask about her? Is there something specific you want me to say if they do?"

Harry breathed out a sigh. "Samantha left when Oliver was eighteen months old, and we haven't seen her since. They know they *have* a mom. She sends Christmas and birthday cards full of cash. And her parents are still around; they see the kids every couple of weeks. They might mention her, but they know the deal. It's not like they're expecting her to show up any day now."

Zoey nodded, her eyes sad. "Got it."

Harry ran a hand through his hair. "She's not a bad person, their mom. She's just not . . . a mom. She wanted a different life."

Zoey shook her head, judgment clouding her expression.

It's not like Harry could blame her. Stepping out on your kids wasn't exactly the honorable thing to do. A year after his divorce, he'd only just started to let go of his bitterness.

"I don't understand," she finally said. "The house, the kids, the dog, the . . ." Her words trailed off and she swallowed, looking Harry up and down, before a trace of pink filled her cheeks.

Harry kept himself from grinning, but silently cheered over her implied meaning. Maybe she was drawn to him as much as he was to her.

"It seems like the kind of life everyone dreams of," Zoey continued.

Harry shrugged. "Not everyone."

She slowly nodded. "I'm sorry, Harry."

He shook his head. "Don't be. Samantha was young when we found out she was pregnant with Hannah. We both were. We got married because it seemed like the right thing to do but raising a kid while I built my career—the first season of *Right-On* aired the year after Hannah was born—it just, it was too hard. I think Oliver was her last-ditch effort to try and make our life into something she wanted, but it did the opposite. I know it makes her sound selfish, but I don't fault her for it. It isn't what she ever wanted for herself. I'd rather she be in New York and happy than here and miserable, making the rest of us miserable too. For my sake, and the kids'."

"What's in New York?" Zoey asked.

"Broadway. Samantha's an actress. She'd landed a pretty big role here in L.A. right before she found out she was pregnant with Hannah and had to back out because of the pregnancy. She decided if she was ever going to make it, she had to be in New York."

"Wow. You have a remarkably generous and mature outlook."

Harry chuckled. "Like I said. It took me more than five years to build this house. That's a lot of therapy."

"Okay. So, no need for tiptoeing around the mom talk, be here between eight and nine, playdates twice a week, dance class for Hannah once a week, and you're home by four every day? Any food allergies I should know about?"

"You got it. And no, no food allergies. Oh, I did forget to mention the SUV in the garage for you to use when you're with the kids. It needs servicing or I'd let you drive it home tonight. I'll take care of it tomorrow, so it'll be ready for you to drive next week. That way, you won't have to worry about moving car seats around or anything."

She nodded. "Sounds great."

Later that night, after he'd taken Zoey home, picked up In-N-Out for dinner and put the kids to bed, Harry collapsed onto the couch in the living room, too tired to do much more than sit there. His life *did* require a lot of juggling. It was worth it; he recognized how fortunate he was to have healthy kids, a job he loved that allowed him to be as involved with his kids as he wanted to be, and a pretty stellar support network with his sister and two sets of grandparents close by. But it would be nice to have a little something for himself mixed in there too. A dating life, for one. Even just a day at the beach for some good surfing without having to worry about the waves eating his children. He suddenly wondered if Zoey surfed. She'd moved from Chicago, but if he remembered correctly, she'd grown up here. Maybe he'd find a way to ask her on Monday morning.

He took his phone from his pocket and pulled up the text thread she'd started that afternoon, when she'd programmed herself into his contacts. She'd sent a single text to herself with nothing but his name, *Harry Beckford.* The fact that she'd called him Harry instead of Harrison made him unreasonably happy. She'd chosen to think of him as friend Harry. Dad Harry. Handyman Harry. Not TV-star *Harrison*.

Could he text her and ask if she liked to surf? Was there a way to bring it up in a way that made it seem pertinent to her working with the kids?

He tossed the phone onto the cushion beside him. Probably not.

The phone suddenly dinged with an incoming text and he scrambled to grab it, somehow hoping that Zoey was reading his mind and voluntarily texting him the answer to his question.

The text didn't mention surfing, but it *was* from Zoey.

Look how pretty! the text read. It was followed by a photo of her closet, fully organized, shoes lined up in neat rows, clothes stacked in the canvas storage bins he'd left for the lower shelves.

It looks amazing, he texted back. *You didn't waste any time putting the space to good use.*

I have a lot of shoes, she texted back. *They needed a home. Plus, organization makes me ridiculously happy.*

You and Hannah will get along great. Her ponies live in color-coordinated bins. He cringed after he hit send, thinking the best way to woo a woman probably wasn't to keep talking about his kids. But then, somehow, he felt like Zoey wasn't the kind of woman who would care.

I knew she was my kind of girl. Thanks again for your help today. And for the job. The dots at the bottom of his screen kept blinking so he waited to see what she'd text next.

I'm really glad we met.

His pulse picked up and he rolled his eyes, annoyed that he had so little control over his emotions. He wasn't a fourteen-year-old boy texting his first crush.

Zoey's text could be totally benign. She was glad because she needed a job that was flexible, and she liked kids. That could be all it meant. But the way she'd looked at him today . . .

He keyed out a response. *I'm glad we met too.*

He reread the text before sending. Was that enough? Should he say more? He added, *I've been looking forward to meeting you for a long time.*

No. That was probably too forward. He deleted the second sentence, sending the text with only the original line. It was true. As soon as Ms. Emily had shown him Zoey's picture and started talking about her granddaughter and all the reasons she thought he'd like her, he'd wanted to meet her. But if he came on too strong, he might mess things up for the kids. He *wanted* Zoey to be a great thing for him, but he was *positive* she would be a great thing for his kids, regardless. He couldn't risk screwing that up before it had even begun.

CHAPTER 5

ZOEY PULLED HARRY'S SUV into his driveway a little before eight in the morning. She still hadn't grown used to driving such a fancy car. When Harry had taken her out to the garage on her first day to turn over the keys, she'd almost hit the floor. She'd heard SUV and thought Ford Explorer, not fully tricked out Porsche Cayenne. The car was easily worth more than a hundred grand.

"Wow," Zoey had said, as she'd stared at the car. "This is the kid car?"

Harry had shrugged but looked chagrined. "It's the only kind of Porsche that makes sense in my life right now."

Two weeks of driving the Porsche and Zoey was convinced it made sense for *her* life, too. She wasn't sure she'd ever be happy behind the wheel of a normal car again. The garage door automatically eased open as she approached, and a silly thrill raced up Zoey's spine. Even that simple convenience—an auto-sensing garage door—still felt exciting.

She pulled out her phone and checked her email one last time before going inside. She tried not to get it out too much when she was with the kids. Harry was paying her generously—she'd asked for double what she would have made fact-checking and he hadn't even hesitated before agreeing to the amount—and she wanted to be as engaged as possible. But she was growing tense for the lack of information coming in from Chicago stations. She'd emailed every producer she knew letting them know she was looking for a new position; she'd updated her LinkedIn profile; she'd done everything she could think to do and still, her inbox was dry.

With a sigh, Zoey dropped her phone into her purse, wishing she'd inherited her father's patience. A therapist by profession, he was all about steady contemplation and giving life the chance to "settle." That's what he would call this jobless period of her life. The chance to reset. To settle in and evaluate her goals. There was probably wisdom in such council for some people, but Zoey didn't need to evaluate anything. She knew her goal. She always had. She would be an evening anchor in Chicago if it was the last thing she did.

Unless no one ever emailed her.

Zoey grabbed the trash left over from the six-dollar latte she'd grabbed on her way home the night before and tossed it into the trash can inside the garage. She locked the SUV behind her, a wave of guilt washing over her as she did. There were worse ways to spend time in between jobs.

Zoey used the number pad by the door to let herself into the house. Harry had insisted the keyless entry was easier than him having to run to the door every morning just to let her in.

Zoey headed toward the kitchen. "Hello?" she called out. The house was unusually quiet.

The kitchen and living room were both empty. Alarm filled Zoey's chest when the kids' bedrooms were empty as well, but then she found the entire family—even Marigold—sound asleep in the master bedroom. Harry was in the middle of his king-sized bed, a kid tucked in on either side of him. A mostly empty bowl of popcorn and several discarded juice boxes littered the floor.

Zoey glanced at her watch. She'd put money on Harry needing to be at work pretty soon. She approached the bed, not wanting to disturb the peaceful scene, but feeling obligated to at least make sure Harry wasn't missing anything important.

A laugh caught in Zoey's throat. Harry's face was covered in make-up. Blue sparkly eye shadow. Bubblegum pink lipstick. Either he'd fallen asleep before Hannah did, or he'd been a really good sport and let her give him a makeover.

Zoey leaned down, gently nudging Harry's shoulder. "Good morning, sleeping beauty," she said softly, not wanting to wake up the kids.

Harry stirred, his eyes slowly drifting open. He looked at Zoey for a long moment before asking, "What time is it?" his voice groggy with sleep.

"A little past eight," Zoey said. Harry jolted into a seated position, his eyes wide.

Zoey lifted a finger to her lips, motioning to the kids on either side of the bed.

He repositioned Oliver to create a little more room for himself, then shimmied down to the foot of the bed where he stood up. "I was supposed to be on set half an hour ago." He ran a hand through his hair, narrowly missing the two pink bows Hannah must have secured the night before.

Zoey bit her lip. Not laughing was getting harder and harder.

Harry picked his phone up off the floor and tried to turn it on. The screen stayed black and he swore.

Zoey stepped forward. "I'll take this and charge it," she whispered, wanting the children to sleep as long as they needed to. "And I'll make you some coffee. You go change."

His shoulders relaxed and he nodded. "Thanks."

Five minutes later Harry stumbled into the kitchen holding his work boots, wearing faded jeans and a light blue flannel the same color as the makeup still gracing his eyelids.

Zoey finished filling a travel mug with coffee, tightening the lid before pulling a washcloth out of a drawer beside the sink and running it under the warm water.

"You'll need this," she said, setting the coffee on the counter next to him. "But not before you use this." She handed him the washcloth.

Harry furrowed his brows. "What for?"

Zoey laughed. "You haven't looked in the mirror yet this morning, have you?"

"I didn't have time." Harry left the kitchen, washcloth in hand, and moved to the entryway where a large mirror hung by the front door.

Zoey followed behind him, not wanting to miss his reaction.

"Wow," he said, when he saw his reflection. "She did good work."

"So I guess this was a 'Daddy's sleeping' makeover and not one you submitted to willingly?"

He rubbed at his face, doing more smearing than anything else. "Why is this not working?"

Zoey stepped closer and pulled the washcloth from his hands. "Here. Stand still. And close your eyes."

Harry followed her instructions, not moving an inch while she rubbed the washcloth over his eyes and lips. His lips . . . she might have lingered there a moment longer than necessary. Had they always looked so kissable?

"We stayed up to watch the new *Frozen* movie," Harry said.

Zoey winced. Harry was standing very close to her.

"Oh no," Harry said, his hand flying to his mouth. "I need to go brush my teeth, huh?"

Zoey smiled sheepishly, hoping that would soften the blow. No one liked being told they had dragon breath. "That would probably be a good idea." She stepped back. "There. You're done."

He nodded, his hand still cupped over his mouth. "Thank you."

He turned to head back to his room, but Zoey stopped him.

"Actually, wait."

He looked back over his shoulder.

Zoey laughed quietly as she reached up and pulled the bows out of Harry's hair. One was tangled in and it took a minute to free the clasp. This part of Harry smelled really good and she felt herself lean in, a pulse of heat running through her body. She suddenly wanted to keep her hands in his hair, slide them down to his shoulders . . .

"Did you get it?" Harry asked, startling her out of the moment.

Zoey took a wide step back. "Yep." She held up the pink bows. "There were two. But I got them."

Harry shook his head as he made his way to his room. "That girl," he muttered under his breath.

A few minutes later, Zoey met him at the front door with the coffee she'd fixed him earlier. He looked as though he'd splashed some water on his face and finger combed his hair as well as brushed his teeth.

"Thank you," he said as he took the mug. "For everything."

Zoey nodded. "Don't worry about it."

"I'm sorry about the morning breath. I'll never stop being embarrassed over that one."

"It happens to everybody," Zoey said with a shrug.

"The kids should sleep a little while longer. And they're going to want to watch *Frozen* again. Oliver had a little bit of a stuffy nose when I tucked him in last night so it might be a good day to just take it easy."

Zoey nodded. "Sounds perfect."

Harry moved his keys and his phone from one hand to the other. "They really love you, Zoe."

Zoey smiled, both at his praise, and at the way he'd shortened her name. "It's completely mutual. I adore being here."

"I don't think they've ever been this content to stay with anyone. I know this probably isn't what you thought you'd be doing when you moved out here, but I want you to know how much I appreciate you."

"Thanks," she said, her voice breaking at the end of the word. She cleared her throat and swallowed. Had he been standing so close to her before?

Zoey had fallen into staring at her boss more than once over the past couple of weeks. She couldn't help it. The guy was next-level good-looking. It probably didn't help matters that in the evenings, she and Nana had started watching Harry's first season of *Right-On Renovations.* So much Harry screen time might be making her slightly obsessed. That she then got to come to his house and see him in person? It definitely helped her obsession along.

Plus, the guy was just. so. charming. He was amazing with his kids, which she'd decided was maybe the sexiest thing she'd ever seen in a man. But he was also amazing with *her.* In the few minutes they were together before and after work, he asked engaging, personal questions, and looked her right in the eyes while she answered, like he cared about what she had to say. He made her feel seen, but in a way that didn't feel as if his attention had anything to do with her looks. She wanted him to find her attractive, and she'd caught an appreciative glance from his direction more than once, so she thought he maybe did. But it never felt like that was *all* he saw when he looked at her.

"I'll see you later?" Harry said, his voice low.

Zoey nodded. "Yeah. Later."

She watched through the sidelights of the front door as he moved down the front walk and climbed into his truck.

Zoey took a deep breath, the first she'd managed in minutes. What was happening to her? She was a woman who had built a career in a high-stress environment; it's why she'd gotten an anchor position so quickly, and while so young. She stayed cool and calm under pressure, she didn't ruffle easily, and she'd handled the curveballs her producers inevitably threw at her without even breaking a sweat. And yet, all Harrison Beckford had to do was say *I'll see you later* and she couldn't even form a coherent sentence.

It wound up being as easy a day as Harry had predicted. Oliver was sleepy all morning which made him particularly snuggly, and Hannah was content to lounge on the couch and read books to them both, in between repeat viewings of *Frozen II*. They popped popcorn and had grilled cheese sandwiches and homemade chocolate chip cookies for lunch, and in the afternoon, they *all* dozed on the couch for close to an hour.

Just before two, Hannah stretched and shifted, knocking a few of the books from the couch onto the floor. "Hey, are we going to Park Play today?"

Zoey kept herself from groaning, but only just. Park Play was a semi-organized weekly play date she'd taken the kids to the week before. They'd had a good time, which was reason enough to go, but Zoey dreaded the hour she'd have to spend sitting around the edges of the park visiting with the other moms. There was actually a place where the moms hung out, and another place where the nannies hung out. But Zoey was Harrison Beckford's nanny. The moms had latched onto her the second she'd shown up and claimed her as one of their own.

Zoey hadn't *really* minded. The moms were nice enough. But their questions had been incessant, and she wasn't comfortable sharing personal details about Harry's life. And they'd never asked about *her* life at all. Nothing about where she was from or what she liked to do had ever entered the conversation. It had been all Harry, all the time.

"Do you want to go?" Zoey asked Hannah. "I'm not sure it's worth waking Oliver up."

Hannah looked at her little brother. "He never sleeps during the day."

"But he was up late last night, and your dad said he had a stuffy nose. He might be fighting a little bit of a bug."

Hannah pursed her lips to the side and scrunched her brow in a way that immediately brought Harry to mind. She didn't exactly *look* like her dad, but that expression was Harry all over. "If we stay here, can we play Uno?"

"Absolutely we can play Uno. As many times as you want."

Uno was a small price to pay to avoid Park Play. At least for one day.

Four rounds of Uno, one game of Candyland, and three puzzles later, Zoey glanced at her watch then looked out the front windows down the long drive that led to the house. Harry had been a few minutes late before, but he was generally pretty good about letting her know if he wouldn't be home by four. He knew she had to be home in time for Cassandra to leave. Once, her first week on the job, he'd anticipated being late enough that he'd called his mom and stepdad and they'd shown up, ready to take over so Zoey could get home. For him to just not show up without any word? There wasn't a precedent for that. Zoey had no idea what to do.

She pulled her phone out of her back pocket, checking one more time for any texts. Biting her lip, she keyed out her own message, pressing send before she could rethink. *Just checking in,* she typed. *Everything okay?*

Hopefully that didn't sound too pushy. It was 4:15. It would only take her five minutes to drive back to Nana's. She didn't need to stress out yet.

When 4:15 turned into 4:45, and then 4:55, she really *did* start to stress. Mostly because Harry hadn't even responded to her text. She'd finally tried to call him after forty-five minutes of waiting, but his phone went to voicemail after two rings. His phone wasn't dead, or it would have gone straight to voicemail without ringing at all; that meant he was probably in some sort of meeting and couldn't answer. Did he go to meetings on a typical workday? In her head, he was always on a job site somewhere, talking to homeowners and filming his show. Of course he had meetings though. *Everyone* had meetings. Acknowledging as much did nothing to solve Zoey's very present dilemma.

She had to be at Nana's house by five, and Harry was nowhere to be found.

Zoey sent a quick message to Cassandra letting her know she'd be late, her frustration fighting with her fear.

"Hey guys?" she called to the kids. They sat at the kitchen table, playing with Play-Doh. "How would you like to go and see Ms. Emily?"

Hannah instantly jumped up. "Can we take her some of the cookies we made today?"

"I bet she'd love that. Good plan. I'll put some in a bag if you can help Oliver get his shoes on."

The kids scurried out of the kitchen, stopping only when Zoey called them back to clean up their mess. That was the normal thing to do. And doing normal things was the only way she could keep herself from worrying. If it was the norm for Harry to be late and noncommunicative, she wouldn't mind taking the kids to Nana's every once in a while. Nana loved seeing the kids. But Harry always called. Or just . . . showed up.

Zoey forced another deep breath as she herded Marigold into her crate, then scooped Oliver up and carried him out to the car, Hannah following behind. It had only been two weeks. Two weeks hardly counted as enough time for there to be a norm. And Harry worked in show business. Was there *any* business less reliable than show business?

She drove the short distance to Nana's house, pausing in the driveway to shoot Harry one more text. *I've got the kids with me at Nana's. I hope you're okay.* She didn't want to be mad at him. Stuff happened. But would it be so hard to respond to a text and let her know he was still alive?

It was almost nine p.m. when Harry finally called.

Zoey answered on the first ring. "Hey," she said, her tone short. "Are you okay?" She shifted a nearly sleeping Oliver from one hip to the other, his arms hanging limply over her shoulders.

"I'm so sorry, Zoey. There was a meeting, and . . . I'm so sorry. Is everyone okay?"

Zoey breathed through her nose, slow and deep, not realizing how tense she'd been with worry until the worry was gone. Now all she felt was anger. "Everyone's fine, but I'm holding Oliver and he's almost asleep. I'll see you when you get here."

Harry paused, then sighed. "I'm sorry," he said again. "I'll see you in forty-five minutes."

Both the kids were finally asleep on Zoey's bed when Harry knocked on Nana's door. She flung the door open, working to keep her anger to a slow simmer, rather than a full-on raging boil.

"Zoey, please let me explain," Harry said.

She folded her arms across her chest, her lips pressed into a tight line.

"The kids are still okay?" he asked. "How's Oliver? Did he go to sleep?"

The concern in his eyes went a long way to soften the edges of Zoey's anger, but she wouldn't let him off the hook that easily. "He's fine. They're both sleeping."

He collapsed against the door jamb and pressed his thumb and forefinger to his temples. "This day has just been . . . we had a problem with a house, with the owners, really. They weren't being completely honest about some things and it . . . it doesn't matter now. We were in this ridiculous meeting with our attorney and their attorney and several network executives. It went so much longer than it was supposed to."

"A meeting so ridiculous you couldn't even call and let me know everything was okay? Take two minutes to respond to a text letting me know you weren't dead somewhere?" Zoey closed her eyes. She sounded like a nagging wife. She wasn't his wife; if she was, she wouldn't want to be the nagging kind. "Sorry. That was rude. I don't mind keeping the kids a few extra hours. I get that stuff happens sometimes. I just wish you'd have let me know. I was starting to imagine the worst."

"I should have called," he said. "You're right about that."

He was her employer, yes. And Zoey wanted to respect that. But she was also doing him a favor. She hadn't moved to California to be a nanny. "Please remember that my first priority has to be my grandmother. It isn't fair to Cassandra, when she's been working all day, to keep her waiting on me. And Nana can't be left alone."

"I get it. I'm sorry."

"Come on," Zoey said, motioning over her shoulder. "I'll

help you get the kids in the car."

They didn't say much as they buckled in the sleeping kids. Zoey balled up Oliver's hoodie and wedged it into the corner of his car seat, turning it into a makeshift pillow.

When she turned away from the car, Harry was right behind her, close enough that her arms brushed up against his chest. She stepped back to avoid him, but with the open car door right behind her, there was nowhere for her to go and she stumbled.

Harry reached for her arm, just above the elbow, stabilizing her as she righted herself. "You okay?" he said, the heat of his fingers searing her skin.

She swallowed. Even her anger wasn't enough to quell the attraction that burned inside her. Why did he have to look *so good*? "I'm good," she said. She shifted to the side, out of Harry's grasp so he could close the door on Oliver's sleeping form. He turned back to face her, his face was drawn and tired. He took a breath like he wanted to say something, but then hesitated and ended up shaking his head instead. "I should get them home."

Zoey stood on the porch, her arms wrapped around herself, and watched as he backed his truck out of the driveway. He lifted his hand in a small wave before pulling forward and disappearing down the road.

Zoey walked back inside, her spirits dim. She wanted to be there for Harry. He was clearly juggling a lot; but that didn't mean she could lose sight of what *she* was juggling. She couldn't compromise on Nana's care. It was the whole reason she'd moved home in the first place. Her entire family was counting on her to be there, to be available, to be *present* in all the ways Nana needed her. She closed and locked the front door, then moved to the living room, settling onto the chair next to Nana's recliner.

"You okay?" Nana said. She looked tired. Her eyes were heavy, and the droop on one side of her face—a consequence of the stroke—looked more pronounced than usual. Cassandra had said it was normal, a result of her fatigue, but it still worried Zoey.

She shrugged. "He says he got caught up in a meeting. I get that things happen, but he should have texted me."

Nana nodded. "He should have. But I'm sure there's an explanation."

Maybe, but Zoey wasn't sure she was in the right frame of mind to hear it. She'd just clocked an unexpected twelve-hour day.

"How are *you*?" Zoey asked. "With the kids here, I haven't had the chance to ask you about your day. You had physical therapy, right? How did that go?"

"I ate some eggs," Nana said.

"Hey!" Zoey squeezed Nana's arm. "That's great."

Nana rolled her eyes. "Oliv—" She stuttered over her words. "Oliver can feed himself eggs."

"It isn't going to last forever, Nana. I promise."

She nodded and managed a smile. "I know. But I'm old enough to have earned the right to complain about it anyway."

Zoey smiled back. "You absolutely have. You can complain to

me anytime you want."

Later, after helping Nana through her evening routine and settling her into bed for the night, Zoey snuggled under her own covers, her laptop open in front of her to binge watch Netflix's latest romcom. She was a sucker for a good romantic comedy. Had been as long as she could remember. It was bad enough when she'd been in college that her roommates had made fun of her constantly. They'd joked that it was such a weird passion when she was studying to become a serious journalist. Zoey had always argued it was exactly *because* her major, and later her work, was so serious and professional. She'd gone into journalism because she loved the importance of sharing the news, of crafting stories that informed and educated viewers clearly and concisely. But the truth was, news was often *bad* news; disasters, political conflict, crime.

What better way to forget the stresses of work than watching a good romance?

An email notification popped up on Zoey's screen and she paused the opening credits of the movie and clicked over to her inbox. The message was from a colleague, a friend really, whom Zoey had worked with when she'd first started out in Chicago.

Zoey's eyes caught on the video thumbnail attached to the bottom of the message.

No freaking way.

Zoey forced her eyes to the top of the message and read each word slowly.

Zoey! Retirement is happening. I repeat. IT. IS. HAPPEN-

ING. And it's happening fast. It was all pretty hush-hush, but I guess Regina is actually being forced into retirement? At least, that's the word on the street. She's working through the end of the summer, but not full time. They're pulling in guest anchors for the next couple of months to cover a few days a week. How soon can you get here? I was on last night, Zoe. ME. Sitting in the evening anchor chair. It was totally surreal. I would love this job so there's a part of me that wants you to stay in California, so I don't have to compete with you. But seriously. I know how bad you've wanted this. At least email them and let them know you didn't fall off the planet and you want a shot. I'll keep you posted on developments on the ground. Enjoy CA. -Veronica

Veronica and Zoey had started as interns at the same station. Work had eventually taken them different directions once they'd finished their internships and they hadn't been super great at keeping in touch. But they still moved in the same circles and were always quick to offer hugs and a quick update whenever they ran into each other. Zoey appreciated that Veronica had even passed on the news about Regina's retirement. She'd had no obligation to pull Zoey into the loop. Though, Veronica knew Zoey well enough to understand how much it would mean for her to have a chance at this job. Veronica and the other interns had always joked there was ambition, and then there was *Zoey*-level ambition. They'd all quickly decided if any of them would make anchor before they were thirty, it would be her.

Zoey did a quick scroll through her inbox. She'd checked in five hundred times the past few weeks. It wasn't possible that she'd missed something. But it surprised her that of everyone she knew in the industry, with all the messages she'd sent and efforts she'd made to stay on the radar of the Chicago news scene, Veronica was the only person that had thought to let her know about the opening. There were producers at Channel 4 that she'd worked with in the past, at least one she was sure she'd emailed when she'd first left town. Had no one besides Veronica thought she'd be interested in the position? Sure she was out of town. But she was only in California; not Siberia.

It was probably pointless, but she dashed off a quick email to the station anyway, assuring them her relocation was only temporary and she'd love to be considered. She attached a couple of reporting clips she was most proud of and sent the message. Maybe that would at least get her in for an interview.

Sighing, Zoey clicked back over to her movie.

Forty-five minutes in, the workaholic main character who had lost her job and returned home to reunite with and fall in love with her old high school boyfriend was snuggled under her covers much as Zoey was. The woman scrolled through Facebook on her phone until she heard a tap on her ground floor window. Because of course she did. That's what happened in romantic comedies. Men threw rocks at windows because that was so much easier than texting.

Movies were dumb.

Zoey watched as the woman opened her window, smiling like a teenager when her love interest told her that he couldn't go another minute without seeing her face.

"Coulda just pulled up her Instagram profile, buddy," Zoey said to herself. Except, then she heard a plink on her *own* window.

Zoey's pulse raced. She was hearing things. *Of course* she was hearing things. Because she *wasn't* the main character in a romantic comedy.

Plink.

Or maybe she was.

She moved to her front window, pushing the curtains aside just as her phone buzzed with a text.

Harry stood in the front yard, his eyes on the phone in his hand.

She lunged back across the room and grabbed her phone, feeling like her heart might explode out of her chest.

Do you think you can let me in? Your neighbor saw me, and I think he's calling the police.

Zoey huffed out a laugh, then tiptoed to the front door, not wanting to wake Nana. She pushed the door open and whisper-yelled across the yard. *"Harry!"*

He looked up and smiled, crossing the distance between them in a few long strides.

She backed into the house and he followed her, closing the front door behind him.

"Hi," Harry said. "Sorry if I pulled you out of bed."

Zoey looked down, suddenly realizing how underdressed she was for a late-night chat with Harrison Beckford. Although, he was pretty casual himself. He wore a pair of Adidas joggers and a hoodie and had a baseball cap pushed low on his forehead. Still, the wide neck of her oversized t-shirt had slipped down over one shoulder, and she wasn't wearing a bra.

She folded her arms across her chest. "Um, hold on. Let me go grab a sweatshirt." She booked it to her room where she grabbed a hoodie out of her closet and pulled it over her head.

"What were you doing out there?" she said, when she returned to the entryway where Harry still stood. She glanced out the sidelights beside the front door. "The neighbor didn't really call the police, did he?"

Harry followed her gaze. "I hope not. I guess we'll know in a minute." Harry nearly buzzed with energy, his eyes bright and his smile wide.

"You could have just texted, you know," Zoey said, matching his smile.

"I did, didn't I? But . . . I don't know. Tossing rocks at your window felt so much more romantic."

Zoey stilled and her eyes dropped to the floor. Romantic? He was *trying* to be romantic?

She looked up through her lashes. "You were going for romance?"

Harry's eyes closed briefly before he shook his head. "No. I mean, yes. But I'm getting ahead of myself. Can we sit somewhere?"

Zoey nodded, realizing she probably ought to have invited him in already. Though, did propriety apply to midnight visits? She was guessing probably not. "Sure." She led him into the living room where she turned on a dim lamp in the corner of the room before dropping onto the couch, motioning for him to join her.

"Where are the kids?" Zoey asked.

"At home with my sister. I bribed her to come and stay with them so I could come see you."

She glanced at the clock on the wall. It really was almost midnight. "That's a good sister."

Harry scoffed. "She's getting a bathroom remodel out of it. I think she's making out fine in this deal."

Zoey's eyes went wide. "You're remodeling her bathroom for this? For coming over here? Seriously, Harry. You could have texted."

"I've owed her a bathroom remodel for months; I just finally agreed to make it happen sooner than later." He lifted his shoulders in a shrug. "Besides, I really did want to see you."

Warmth pulsed through Zoey at his words. "Why is that?" she said, her voice low.

Harry took a deep breath. "I need to apologize."

Zoey cocked her head. "You already did."

"No, I know. I apologized as your employer. And I hope you felt how genuine I was. I shouldn't have inconvenienced you and made you worry. It wasn't fair, it was a bad judgement call on my part, and it won't happen again."

"I get it, Harry. It's okay. I know it must be hard keeping all the plates in the air."

"It *is* hard. But sometimes I get terrible tunnel vision. I have a hard time stepping out of the immediate moment to recognize how my actions might affect other people. Also, and I'm not trying to make excuses here, but the network is . . . sensitive about stuff when it comes to my kids. They've already given me so much room, so much flexibility so that I can be with them as much as I am. I think I already told you they redid the entire production schedule to accommodate me and the kids. I guess it's made me extra sensitive. I hate to even mention Hannah and Oliver when I'm working because I've already asked for and been given so much."

"That makes sense," Zoey said.

"The mood in the meeting was already so tense, I was afraid I would make things worse. In my head, I knew the children were safe with you—I'd seen your texts—so I prioritized keeping the peace with the network because that felt more important at the time. But that's no excuse. That didn't account for how *you* felt."

As far as apologies went, his was pretty good. "Apology accepted," Zoey said. "I promise. I totally get it."

"But see, now I want to apologize not as your employer, but . . . as a man. As a man who realized how much he didn't want you to be mad at him, not because you're his children's nanny, but because of how much he likes you."

Zoey balled her hands into fists so Harry wouldn't see them trembling. This was a moment that beat out the movie she'd been watching by a mile.

"Would you like to have dinner with me, Zoey?"

She opened her mouth to respond, but her words were stuck in her mouth. *Harrison Beckford* had just asked her out on a date. *The* Harrison Beckford. Women adored him. Men idolized him. Little kids wore tool belts and pretended to *be* him. But more than that, he was a guy who clearly loved his kids, doted on her Nana like she was royalty, and had a smile that made her knees feel wobbly. Of course she wanted to have dinner with him. But no matter how much she wanted to, she couldn't go to dinner if it meant leaving Nana. Before the words were out of her mouth, Harry was already addressing her concerns.

"I know you can't leave Ms. Emily, but I was thinking, maybe I could come here. Pick up some take-out for the three of us? I'll get my parents to stay with the kids." His shoulders lifted and fell, as if he'd accomplished no small task in getting the words out. "What do you think?"

Oh, Zoey was so far gone for this guy. Boldly, she reached over and wrapped her fingers overtop of his; he turned his hand, opening his palm so their fingers intertwined. She bit her bottom lip, hardly able to suppress her smile. "I think I'm really, *really* glad you asked."

CHAPTER 6

HARRY STOOD IN THE entryway of his home and readjusted his collar, wondering if a button-down shirt was too dressy. He was only having dinner at Ms. Emily's house. It's not like he was taking Zoey somewhere fancy. But it was still a date, even if an unusual one. If he went too casual, would he make Zoey think he wasn't serious about it? Like it was just dinner among friends?

If he was certain about anything, it was that he did not want Zoey to be his friend. She charmed him, intrigued him, excited him in ways that he'd never experienced. Which was saying something. He'd been *married* and wasn't sure he'd ever felt anything quite like this. Though, even in the few short weeks she'd been working for him, Zoey had done more *wife*-like things than Samantha ever had. She noticed him, cared about him, cared *for* him. He felt seen in ways that he never had before.

He wasn't the kind of guy that bought into the idea of soulmates, and it was way too early to use big words like the *L* word. But instead of just feeling like things *could* work with Zoey if they were to date, it felt more like they were *meant* to, like fate was propelling them forward as much as mutual attraction.

Or maybe it was all in Harry's head and Zoey would race back to Chicago if she had any idea how serious his thoughts had turned. He ran a hand through his hair, brushing the long-ish parts on top to the side, and gave his head a little shake.

"Time for a haircut," his mom said from behind him.

He turned.

She leaned against the wall, her arms folded across her chest and a warm smile on her face. "You look nice, Harry. You don't have anything to worry about."

Hannah rounded the corner at a full run and slammed into Harry's legs, wrapping her arms around his knees. He reached a hand out for the wall, stabilizing himself against the impact. "Whoa, slow down. You're going to knock me over."

"Bye, daddy," Hannah said. "Have fun on your date."

Harry crouched down and looked Hannah in the eye. "Thanks, Han. You help your grandma with Oliver, okay?"

She nodded. "Tell Zoey I said hi and not to forget Mr. Brown Bear when she comes over tomorrow cause I left him at Ms. Emily's house and sleeping without him was so terrible."

"Got it," Harry said. "Or I could bring Mr. Brown Bear home with me tonight."

He'd debated whether or not to be honest with Hannah about the fact that he was going on a date with Zoey. Hannah had seen him leave on dates before, but the situation was slightly different because Hannah knew Zoey so well. In the end, he'd decided honesty was the easiest route forward. His kids were with Zoey so much, the idea of keeping secrets, especially when Hannah was generally so perceptive, felt like too much work.

"Oh, do that, Daddy! Then I can sleep with him tonight!"

Harry gave his daughter one more quick hug. "You'll be asleep before I get home, but I'll for sure bring Mr. Brown Bear into your room and tuck him in beside you so you'll have him in the morning when you wake up."

Harry's stepdad joined them in the entryway, Oliver in his arms. Oliver reached out for his dad and Harry scooped him up, giving him a quick squeeze before passing him back to his grandfather. Was it always so much work to get out of the house?

He backed toward the door, grabbing his keys off the entryway table. "I'll see you guys later, okay?" When he was finally settled in the cab of his truck, he took a deep breath, momentarily leaning his forehead against the steering wheel.

Maybe he was crazy.

His life certainly was. Who was he to think he could manage dating someone when it took ten minutes of saying goodbye just to leave his kids for three hours?

Sighing, he cranked the car and drove the short distance to the Japanese restaurant where he'd placed a to-go order. His assistant had offered to pick up the food and bring it by, so he wouldn't have to pick it up himself. It had been tempting.

He didn't generally mind interacting with fans and the general public when people recognized him, but it took time—time he'd rather be spending with Zoey. But his assistant, Jason, was the worst workaholic; just because he was willing to fill his evenings doing stuff for Harry didn't mean Harry wanted him to have to do it. Harry's work/home boundaries when it came to his own family time were nonnegotiable. He wouldn't infringe on Jason's evenings because he was too spoiled to pick up his own dinner.

Harry stepped into the dim interior of the restaurant and made eye contact with the hostess. She gave him a slight nod of acknowledgement, enough to tell Harry she knew who he was, and she'd be with him momentarily. Harry pulled out his phone and leaned against the wall while he waited.

Moments later, a woman stepped up beside him, slipping her hand over his forearm and pulling her body close. "Hi. I'm sorry to bother you, but you're Harrison Beckford."

Harrison very gently tugged his arm away, offering enough of a smile that the woman wouldn't be offended. Greta, his publicist, had explained to him once that fans didn't mean to violate boundaries of personal space. They would never do as much to total strangers. But their favorite celebrities didn't *feel* like strangers. They felt like friends, like people they hung out with on the weekends. "Your face is on their television every day, Harrison," she had said. "I'm not saying you have to have dinner with them, and you're welcome to reestablish boundaries however you see fit. Just do it politely. They're the reason you have a job, after all."

"Hi," Harrison said to the woman. "How are you?"

She closed her eyes and took a deep breath. "Oh my word. It is you, and you just asked me how I am. I really love your show."

"Thank you. I appreciate that." Harry noted over the woman's shoulder that the hostess was approaching, two large to-go bags in her hands. She held them up, nodding her head as they made eye contact.

"Do you think I can get a selfie with you?" the woman asked.

Harry forced a smile. "Sure. But just one. It looks like my order is ready to go."

After smiling into the woman's phone, keeping his body as far away from hers as possible despite her best efforts, he grabbed his food, tipped the hostess, and hurried toward his truck.

"A nice dinner at home tonight, mate?" A voice called from across the parking lot. Harry sighed. He really should have taken Jason up on his offer. He turned and saw a photographer capturing shots of him as he unlocked his truck. He'd been targeted by the paparazzi before but picking up dinner to-go on a random Saturday night wasn't generally something that caught their radar. There wasn't supposed to be anyone that knew where he'd planned to be tonight. More anxious to get away than to figure out *how* the photographer had tracked him down, Harry climbed into his truck and revved the engine, ignoring the man's continued attempts to get a comment from him.

After pulling the truck into Ms. Emily's driveway, he pulled out his phone, sending a quick text to Greta before going inside. *Any idea why the paparazzi knew where I was grabbing dinner tonight?*

The little dancing dots at the bottom of the text thread immediately started bouncing so he waited for a reply. *Where were you?*

Red Ginger in Santa Monica.

You and every other celebrity who wants to be seen, Greta texted back. *You're asking for it going to Red Ginger.*

Really? When did that happen?

When Jessica Appleton told Instagram it was her new favorite.

Harry sighed. *Am I supposed to know who that is?*

They're calling her the next Julia Roberts.

I'm just bitter she ruined my favorite restaurant.

Isn't that why you have Jason? Why are you picking up your own dinner anyway?

He does too much after hours already, Harry texted back.

Then join this century and use Grubhub.

Harry sighed. Why didn't he think of Grubhub? *Fine. Point taken.*

Were you at least nice to the photographer? Greta asked.

Once, right after Harry's divorce, a photographer had gotten right in his face while he'd been out with his children. He'd been in a terrible mood, having just left a meeting with his attorney and had not so kindly pushed—some say *shoved*—the guy to the side so he could get Hannah into the car safely. His actions had created a small media storm for Greta to handle. The tabloids were full of *Angry after his divorce* headlines for weeks, citing the incident and doing their best to dig up stories from homeowners and contractors he'd worked with over the years willing to claim he had an anger management issue. It was all fabricated—it was amazing what people were willing to say when a little bit of cash was up for grabs—and Greta had handled things like the professional that she was. But she'd also scolded him and reiterated his responsibility to keep himself under control. It was a difficult balancing act—respecting and appreciating the public that had helped build his career while also demanding the privacy his family deserved. He was welcome to demand that privacy, but he couldn't push people in the process.

I didn't say a word, Harry texted back. *Just ignored him.*

Good job, Greta responded.

The whole thing made Harry tired. He loved his job. Loved the life it provided for him and his kids. But there was a downside to fame. He wondered if Zoey was the kind of woman who would want to endure it. She'd had a small taste of living her career in the limelight, working as a news anchor. So the scene wasn't completely foreign to her. He could only hope she would understand, that she'd think he was worth any negative side effects his fame brought. But he was getting ahead of himself. He didn't doubt the chemistry that flared between him and Zoey; he had enough experience reading women to know that she was feeling the same thing he was. But she was only in town temporarily. He couldn't start thinking long term before they'd even had their first date.

He thought about the way her hand had so naturally slipped into his and fire flared in his gut. Maybe he couldn't think about the future just yet, but he wouldn't stop himself from looking forward to tonight.

Zoey pulled the door open before Harry had even had the chance to knock. Her hair lay in loose waves on her shoulders and she wore dark jeans and a white flowy shirt. She was dressier than she normally was when she showed up every morning, and he was suddenly glad he'd made a little bit of an extra effort himself. They'd said casual, but he wanted her to know he cared. That he wanted to impress her.

"Hi," Zoey said, her eyes bright. "Come on in."

Harry stepped into the doorway and paused in front of Zoey. "Hey," he said, his voice low. She smelled good. *Really* good. She'd put some kind of gloss on her lips that drew his eye, filling him with a sudden desire to lean in and kiss her right there, while he still held the boxed-up food and hadn't even closed the front door behind him.

She motioned toward the kitchen. "Come on. Nana's already at the table."

Harry followed Zoey into the kitchen, noticing the way her jeans accentuated her curves. He acknowledged, not for the first time, how effortless she made it all look. She looked good, but she didn't look like she was *trying* to look good. It was the kind of sexy he appreciated. "I got a little bit of everything," Harry said. "I hope that's okay."

"It smells amazing," Ms. Emily said.

Harry watched as Zoey dished up a plate of food for her grandmother, assembling an array of things on her plate that looked easy to spear with a fork. No noodles, or slippery vegetables. "Want to give it a try?" She shifted the plate closer to Ms. Emily and held out a fork.

Ms. Emily took a deep breath. "No chopsticks for me?"

Zoey glanced at Harry, her expression slightly panicked, but Nana quickly put them all at ease. "I'm kidding," she said. "I'm not *that* ambitious." She looked at Harry and picked up her fork. "I'm going to make a mess, Harry. I'm just warning you now."

Harry smiled. "It's a shame Oliver isn't here. He'd probably make a contest out of it."

Ms. Emily rolled her eyes. "Ha. He might be the only one that could beat me."

Dinner went by fast, punctuated by multiple long looks shared with Zoey across the table and enough laughing to reiterate Harry's belief that he'd actually met the perfect woman.

After dessert—some sort of chocolate sushi thing that was maybe the best dessert Harry had ever tried—they moved to the living room and watched recorded episodes of *Wheel of Fortune* and *Jeopardy*, Zoey sitting next to him on the couch, until Ms. Emily started to fall asleep in her chair.

Zoey reached out and put a hand on his knee. "I'm going to help Nana get to bed."

"Oh." Harry nodded. "Should I . . . go?" *Please say no.*

Zoey shook her head, making him smile. "It'll only take a half-hour or so. Can you wait for me?"

Harry grinned. "Absolutely."

Before Zoey could help Ms. Emily out of her chair, Harry stood up and leaned down to give the older woman a hug, kissing her softly on the cheek.

"That better not be the only kissing that happens tonight," Ms. Emily said with a twinkle in her eye.

"Nana!" Zoey said, but Harry only laughed.

"What? You think I don't see the way you two have been looking at each other? I was worried you might not wait for me to go to bed."

Zoey pushed her forehead into her palm. "What am I going to do with you?"

"It's like being in high school all over again," Harry said. "Except maybe worse." He met Zoey's eye and she smiled.

"Definitely worse."

Harry settled back onto the couch and pulled out his phone to check on his kids while he waited. His mom assured him everything was fine; the kids were settled, and he was welcome to stay out as long as he wanted. He glanced over and caught sight of Mr. Brown Bear, sitting in the corner of the armchair next to him. He reached over and grabbed it, not wanting to forget it when he finally left, then turned back to his phone, the bear tucked onto his lap.

"Did you get lonely without me?" Zoey asked, moving back

into the room twenty minutes later.

Harry looked down at the bear and smiled. "I did. This guy's a poor substitute though. His jokes aren't funny at all."

Zoey plopped onto the cushion next to him and propped her elbow up on the back of the couch, her chin resting on her fist. "Maybe he doesn't like you. He tells me the best stories when you aren't around."

Harry lifted up the bear and frowned. "Whatever happened to family loyalty, huh?"

Zoey laughed, a sound he would love to hear again and again. "First the kids, now Mr. Brown Bear. You better watch out. I'm going to make everyone in your family convinced they can't live without me and then where will you be?"

Harry stilled, leveling her a look that he hoped wasn't too serious. "Doesn't sound like such a bad deal if you ask me."

She scrunched her nose as if to disagree. "I don't know, Harry. There's a lot you don't know about me. I can think of ten things right off the top of my head that might make you change your mind."

The gleam in her eye made Harry think her ten things might make him like her more. "Try me."

"What? All ten things on the first date? What kind of a strategist would I be if I gave you *all* my secrets in one night? I mean, I have to at least get a few more free meals out of this deal."

"It's all about the food with you, isn't it?"

She bit her bottom lip and smiled. "You just guessed secret number four."

"Lucky for you, I love food too. Cooking it, buying it, especially eating it."

"How often do you eat dessert?" Zoey asked as she stood from the couch. She walked across the room and opened a drawer on a small side table.

"Is this a trick question?" Harry asked. He was all about dessert. But he also had an agent that frequently reminded him how important his physique was to his image on the show.

"Not a trick question," Zoey said. "Definitely a test question, though." She held something behind her back, but Harry couldn't see what it was.

"When I'm hitting the gym like I'm supposed to be, or I'm in between seasons, I will always eat dessert. When I'm filming, and I'm not working out regularly, I'm a little more disciplined."

Zoey rolled her eyes.

"That's not fair!" Harry said playfully. "It's in my contract."

"Seriously?! Dessert restrictions are in your contract?"

Harry ran a hand through his hair, suddenly wishing he hadn't brought it up. It was the thing he hated the most about his job. It was never just about remodeling houses. It was about remodeling houses while he was wearing just the right shirt to match the blue of his eyes *and* accentuate his biceps. "Not dessert. But . . ." He waved his hand down the length of his body.

"Ohhhh," Zoey said, almost gleeful. She danced back across the room. "So it's the muscles that are in the contract." She sat back down on the couch, dropping a deck of cards on the coffee table in front of them before wrapping both arms around his bicep. "I've got to admit. I think I support your contract."

This time, Harry rolled his eyes before shrugging out of her grip. He caught her hands in his. "Yeah, yeah. What about you? How do you feel about dessert?"

"Can't live without it," Zoey answered, almost immediately. "And since I am genetically fortunate enough to have an incredibly fast metabolism, I don't ever have to."

"That *is* fortunate." He looked at the cards and raised his eyebrows. "What are the cards for?"

"The cards have to do with the first thing on my list."

"Wait. Do you actually have a list?"

She grinned. "No. But if I did, this would definitely be the thing on the top."

Harry narrowed his eyes. "You . . . like to gamble?"

She shook her head.

"You build card houses in your spare time."

She leaned her head against the couch and pretended to snore.

"Fine. I cave. What's the thing most likely to scare me away?"

She opened the cards and pulled out the deck, shuffling them in her hands. "I am *extremely* competitive."

"That's it? I think that's a good thing."

"No, you don't understand. Like, when I play Candyland with Hannah, it takes *all* of my willpower not to pout when she beats me and brag when I beat her. Like, I have to remind myself over and over that I'm an adult and she's a kid and I know better."

"Over Candyland?" Harry said.

"A game's a game," Zoey said. "I mean, I won't behave badly over it. But I really like to win."

Harry looked back to the cards. So far, he'd been right. The stuff she thought might scare him off *did* make him like her more. "So we're going to play a game?"

Her lips lifted in a sly smile. "Only if you're up for it."

A rush of energy pulsed through him. Oh, he was up for it. A thousand times yes, he was up for it.

CHaPTer 7

"SO HERE'S HOW IT'S going to go," Zoey said. She scooted back on the couch so the cushion between them was bare. "The game is called Speed. It's a little like double solitaire, except faster, and with fewer cards."

"Sounds fun," Harry said. She looked up, happy to see that his facial expression matched the tone of his voice. It was an impulse decision to pull out a deck of Nana's cards, but she was having too much fun bantering with Harry to do something as boring as watching a movie. She loved that he'd spar with her a little, toss jokes back at her as fast as she threw them to him. It was a side she hadn't seen of him before and she liked it. *Really* liked it.

She finished explaining the rules to Harry, walking him through a practice round until he'd grasped the rules.

"Got it," he said. "So we play until one of us gets rid of all of our cards?"

"Yep. That's the goal." She hesitated. There *was* a way they could make the game more interesting. Zoey had long since learned that sometimes her playful side got her into trouble, but Harry had been giving her signs all night. She'd caught him staring at her lips more than once; he wanted to kiss her. She took a breath. Once she posed her next question, there was no going back. "Care to up the stakes a little?" She kept her tone teasing.

Harry cocked his head to the side. "How so?"

"The winner of each round gets to give the loser a kiss, but the kiss can't be on the lips. Not until someone has won the entire game."

Harry grinned. "I like the way you play, Zoey Williamson."

Zoey took the first round without even having to try. She'd had lucky cards, but Harry was also slow. She was probably going to be giving lots of kisses before the night was over. That meant she needed to start slow. She reached for Harry's hand and held it with hers, massaging the sides of his palm just slightly before raising it up and planting a chaste kiss on the pad of his thumb.

Still, she watched his Adam's apple bob as he swallowed. "Round two," he said, his voice slightly huskier than it had been before.

Round two was another win for Zoey, and a kiss on the inside of Harry's wrist. Round three Zoey won before Harry played a single card. For such a demoralizing loss, she graduated up to his cheek, lingering close to his face long enough to say, "You better not be losing on purpose."

"It's my first time playing the game," he argued. "And you're crazy fast. It's not a fair fight and you know it."

Zoey shrugged. "It's just as much luck as it is skill."

Harry scoffed. "Says the girl who always wins."

Zoey only smiled, shuffling her dwindling cards one more time before laying out round four.

"Ha!" Harry said a few minutes later when he finally won. "Take that!"

He was proud enough of himself that Zoey didn't even mind he'd ruined her clean sweep.

Harry leaned forward and she froze, her heart jumping into her throat. He hovered over her, close enough for her to smell his aftershave, feel the tickle of his breath on her cheek. He lifted his hand and slowly slid her hair back away from her neck, his fingers brushing lightly against her skin.

Zoey closed her eyes, goose flesh rising up and down her arms. Harry's lips touched the corner of her jaw, just below her ear. Her breath caught. She wrapped her fingers around the hem of her shirt, knowing if she didn't hold on to something else, she'd definitely start holding onto him. "I hope *you* didn't lose on purpose," he whispered, before settling back onto his side of the couch.

Zoey finally opened her eyes. "I didn't, but if you promise the next kiss will be that good, I will."

He grinned. "Nope. We're playing fair and square or not at all."

It took six more rounds; four wins for Zoey, and two for Harry before Zoey was down to her final three cards—two aces and a king. Zoey watched, her muscles tense, as Harry flipped over card after card, none of them cards she could actually play on. Finally, Harry turned over a two and Zoey flew into action, laying down an ace, then a king, then her final ace of the game. Instead of throwing her hands up in the air in a customary shout of victory, Zoey stilled, her gaze locked on Harry. "I won," she said, her voice subdued. She swallowed.

Harry's eyes shone with warmth. "Yes, you did."

Zoey shifted across the couch until she sat on her knees in front of him, her heart pounding, caring little for the cards she sent careening onto the floor. She lifted her hands to either side of his face, sliding them back to his hairline, then down to his shoulders. She leaned close, her lips hovering over his, but didn't complete the kiss.

"You're doing this on purpose," Harry said, laughter in his voice.

"Don't ruin my victory lap," Zoey said. Finally, she closed the distance, pressing her lips to his. He awakened to the contact, his hands wrapping around her back. Zoey couldn't get enough of the man in front of her—the smell of him, the taste of him, the feel of his arms holding her to him.

Harry groaned in a way that made Zoey's blood heat before his hands slid up and into her hair. He turned his head just slightly, deepening the kiss. Zoey melted into his touch, but willed herself to breath, to keep herself grounded.

When their lips finally parted, Zoey could feel the smile on Harry's face. "Actually, I think I'm the winner," he said.

Zoey leaned forward and kissed him one more time. "I really like you, Harry Beckford."

Harry's phone buzzed with an incoming text, vibrating against the coffee table where he'd placed it before their game. Harry didn't reach for it, but Zoey sensed she'd lost a fraction of his attention.

She motioned to the phone with her head. "Go ahead," she said.

His shoulders dropped in obvious relief. "Sorry. I need to make sure it isn't anything about the kids."

Zoey smiled, shifting positions to give Harry room to check his phone. Still, she left her arm wrapped through his, her head leaning against his shoulder.

"It *is* the kids. Mom says Oliver has a fever."

"Oh, no. Is he okay?"

Harry stood up. "She says it's really high. I think I need to go."

Zoey nodded. "Of course. Go!" Zoey followed him to the door, scooping up Mr. Brown Bear from the floor on her way. "Don't forget this," she said, offering the stuffed animal to Harry.

He tucked it under his arm, then reached for Zoey, wrapping his other arm around her waist and pulling her against him. "You know what? This is the best first date I've ever had."

A zing of energy pulsed through Zoey. "Me too." She leaned

up on her toes and kissed him one more time, her hand lingering on the curve of his jaw. "Will you text me and let me know how Oliver's doing? I don't care how late it is."

"For sure."

"And if Hannah needs to come hang out with me and Nana tomorrow, she's welcome."

Harry shook his head. "I don't want you to have to work on a Sunday, Zoe."

"I wouldn't be working. I'd be helping out a . . . friend." She bit her lip. It was too soon to call him a boyfriend, but it wasn't hard to imagine herself saying the word.

"Thank you." He kissed her again. "And thanks again for tonight."

Zoe practically floated back to the living room. She dropped to the floor, picking up the scattered cards from her victory make-out session.

Harrison Beckford was a very good kisser.

Cards cleaned up, Zoey dropped onto the couch and relived their kisses like she was a high school sophomore, right down to the cheesy grin on her face. Her phone rang from the side table beside the couch and she reached for it. It couldn't be Harry. He'd only just left, but a part of her wished it was all the same.

Nana's image filled the screen on Zoey's phone, which made emotions of an entirely different sort swell inside her. "Nana?" she answered. "Are you okay?" Zoey was at her grandmother's bedroom door before Nana had even had the chance to reply. Zoey pushed it open to see her grandmother propped up against her headboard, the small lamp by her bedside casting a warm circle of yellow light onto her pillow.

Nana smiled when she saw Zoey and ended the call. "Well?" she said expectantly.

Zoey rolled her eyes but smiled before climbing onto the bed beside her grandmother. "You about gave me a heart attack. I thought something had happened to you."

"What could happen to me while I'm in my bed? I want you to tell me about your night with Harry."

Zoey sighed and leaned against the tufted headboard, not even sure where to begin.

"That good, huh?" Nana said.

Zoey chuckled. "Seriously. He might be perfect, Nana. He's so nice. And funny. And so sweet to his kids, and let me tell you, I never thought about that being particularly sexy but seeing it in action? Um, yes. It's maybe the hottest thing ever. He's smart. Witty. And he jokes with me. I mean, I knew he was charming because I've watched his show, but in person, it's so much more than that."

"And there's physical attraction, too? Good chemistry?"

Zoey grunted her response, a visceral reaction that sounded like a weird cross between a moan and the guttural noise of a motorcycle revving its engine. It even surprised Zoey and she laughed, her hand flying to her mouth.

"Wow," Nana said. "I guess I should say you're welcome."

Zoey tilted her head to look Nana in the eye. "It makes me a little scared, you know? For it to feel this good." She lifted her shoulders in a shrug. "Like it could be too good to be true."

Nana patted her hand. "Just take it one day at a time."

Zoey nodded and took a deep breath. "Yeah. That's good advice."

"Would you move out here for him? Permanently?"

Zoey pondered the question. It was technically too soon to even think about it. They were one kiss in. Or, one *night* of kissing in. She couldn't make such a huge decision based on that. But she'd be lying to herself if she pretended like she couldn't envision a future for herself in California, a life with Harry and his kids.

At the same time, if she got a call from Channel 4 News in Chicago offering her an anchor position, she'd take it without even pausing to think about it. She wasn't sure what that meant about what her heart really wanted. Probably that her heart didn't have a clue.

"I don't know," she finally answered. "My life is in Chicago. My career. My family. I mean, except for you, of course. I'd always love being closer to you."

Nana squeezed her hand in understanding. Zoey's family had long since given up on trying to convince Nana to move to Chicago to be closer to her family. She had always refused, insisting she'd never sacrifice a house that was paid for and a near perfect climate to be buried in snow half of the year. She was as much a Californian as Zoey was a Chicagoan.

"But with Harry, you could have a family. Kids of your own."

A worry wormed into the back of Zoey's mind. It didn't have

to be just one or the other, did it? A career, or a family? Zoey's mom had never had a career outside the home. She'd raised her kids, then mothered her adult children from afar until Zoey's brother, Nathan, had gotten married and had a set of twins. He and his wife were both teachers and as soon as the babies were born, Mom had practically begged Nathan to let her keep the kids during the day. She'd been a good example for Zoey and had always been encouraging in her own way. But Zoey couldn't help but feel like her mother didn't actually think her life would start until she was married and having kids. Her career was just a placeholder, a thing to do until she'd met the right man.

In a lot of ways, the unspoken pressure had pushed Zoey the opposite direction, making her fight even harder to build her career. She didn't need a man to be happy, and she would prove it.

But in her heart, she *did* want to be married. To have kids someday.

Surely there was a way she could have both.

She sat up and squeezed Nana's hand. "Maybe you're all the California family I really need."

Nana scoffed. "The sound you made a minute ago leads me to think you need a lot more than an old woman to keep you company." She raised her eyebrows playfully and gave Zoey a knowing grin.

"Nana, you're terrible."

"I'm old, Zoey. Not dead."

Zoey's phone dinged with an incoming message when she

was brushing her teeth to get ready for bed. Sure it was from Harry, anticipation filled her as she finished up, grabbing the phone and climbing into bed before she opened the text.

It was a picture of Harry in his bed, a sleeping Oliver up against his chest. The light was dim, but Zoey could still see the pink tinge to Oliver's cheeks and see the damp curls clinging to his forehead. The picture only showed the bottom half of Harry's face, but it nicely accentuated the shape of his shoulder and arm as it cradled his son.

"Oh, my freaking heart," Zoey said out loud. The caption read, *Fever broke and he's sleeping with me for the night. Long live acetaminophen.*

Jealous, Zoey typed out. But no. Now was not the time for flirting. The man had a sick kid in his arms. Zoey deleted the word to try again. *I'm so glad,* she wrote. *I love his little face.* There. Totally appropriate.

I had a good time tonight, his next message read.

Zoey couldn't stop smiling. *Me too.*

I might have to find a reason to see you before Monday morning.

Monday morning is only thirty-six hours away. And you have a sick kid.

Both true statements. Still doesn't change the way I feel. He followed the message with a winking smiley face. Before she could respond, one more message popped up. *Good night, Zoey. Sleep well.*

Zoey dropped her phone onto her chest and closed her eyes.

This wasn't happening. *He* wasn't happening. She could almost squeal for how surreal it all felt. Steadying her hands, she picked up her phone and texted him back. *Good night, Harry.* Feeling slightly bold, she followed her message with an intentional, purpose-filled bright red heart.

CHAPTER 8

HARRY PUSHED HIMSELF UP from the breakfast table and grabbed his plate, carrying it to the sink where he rinsed it off and loaded it into the dishwasher. He moved back to the table and kissed each of his kids, then wrapped his arms around Zoey's waist from behind and rested his chin on her head. Hannah watched him the entire time; she smiled when he caught her eye before looking back to her pancakes.

Zoey leaned into him, turning her head slightly. "I wish you didn't have to work today," she said.

"Me too."

She swiveled in his arms until they stood face to face. It had only been a few weeks since they'd started dating, but seeing her in his house, with his kids, every single day had brought a familiarity to their relationship much faster than he guessed would have happened had he just been taking her out on a date every once in a while.

"So we're meeting back at Nana's this afternoon, right?"

Harry nodded. "I'll be there by four. I've got to go by Charlotte's house to finish up the tile in her shower, but Tyson already did most of the install, so it shouldn't take me long."

"Tyson? From your show, Tyson?" Zoey asked.

Harry nodded. "Yeah. He does great tile work."

Zoey wrinkled her brow. "I think a part of me thought the work you guys do on TV is all staged. Like you bring in tradesmen to do the actual work, and then the pretty faces get to pretend they were the ones that did it for the camera."

"I'm going to try hard not to be insulted by your assumptions."

Zoey grinned. "I never thought *you* were faking. You seem like the real deal. Plus, I've seen your truck and your tools and this house, which I know you built all by yourself. But Tyson is just so pretty. He seems like he ought to be modeling underwear instead of installing tile."

Harry chuckled. "I'll be sure and tell him you said so."

Zoey swatted him on the chest. "You will not."

"Everybody on the show knows what they're doing and could absolutely do the entire job if they had to. What viewers don't see is that it's never *just* the pretty face that's doing all the work. We complete projects way too fast to get it done with only the people you see on screen. There's probably two dozen people that are also on the crew, working in the background around the clock so that we stay on schedule." It was that crew that made it possible for Harry to have such a flexible schedule, so he'd never stop singing their praises. He was lucky. The network could have said no when he'd demanded after his divorce that he have regular work hours and evenings with his kids. Had he not built up such a reliable crew of skilled craftsmen, they might not have been so willing.

"So Tyson's pretty face *does* have something to do with why he's the one on camera and not just working behind the scenes."

Harry shrugged. He'd stand by Tyson's work any day, but Zoey wasn't wrong. "America does love a pretty face."

Zoey's hands slipped up his arms. "We already know your biceps are a part of your contract, so I guess that isn't surprising."

Harry closed his eyes briefly, loving the feel of Zoey's fingers grazing against his skin. Everything still felt so new, he almost couldn't believe she was real. That she liked him. Liked his kids.

"You're making leaving really hard," he whispered.

She grinned. "That's the goal."

"Kiss her goodbye, Daddy!" Hannah called from the kitchen table.

Harry looked back to Zoey, motioning with his head toward Hannah. "I think she's your second-biggest fan."

Zoey raised an eyebrow. "Second-biggest?"

Harry leaned forward and kissed her gently. "Nobody likes you more than I do."

Later, Harry leaned against the kitchen counter at Charlotte's, drinking a cup of coffee while she rolled out cinnamon roll dough on the counter. He hadn't seen much of his sister since Zoey had started staying with his kids and he missed talking to her.

"So I guess things with Zoey are still going well?" she said. "You never did tell me if she accepted your apology that night you dragged me out of bed so you could go see her."

Harry stilled, suddenly realizing that he'd never told Charlotte he and Zoey had started dating. He ran a hand through his hair. How had he failed to mention it? It had been so late when he'd returned home that night that Charlotte had quickly left to get back to her own family before they'd really even talked. Then he'd just been . . . busy.

"Oh. Um, yeah. She accepted my apology. Things are good."

"Good." Charlotte pulled the brown sugar out of the cabinet.

The fact that she didn't say anything more almost worried Harry. Charlotte had been badgering him about Zoey since he'd first mentioned Emily's desire that he date her granddaughter. Char had jumped on board immediately, having long since decided it was time for him to start dating again. But now she wasn't even going to ask a follow-up question? Ask if he liked her? Something was up.

Harry glanced at his watch. He didn't have time to wait for the rolls to be done, not if he wanted to make it to Emily's in time to meet Zoey and the kids. But Charlotte's rolls might be worth making a second trip. Especially if he couldn't get her to talk this time around.

Charlotte sprinkled the sugar over the melted butter that covered the dough, a weariness in her movements that Harry hadn't noticed before.

"Hey, Char, you okay?"

She looked up. "What? Yeah."

"You look a little tense. And tired."

She scoffed. "Thanks for the compliment."

"And you haven't asked a single question about me and Zoey. We're dating. And I really like her."

She turned to face him, wiping her sugar-covered fingers on a dish towel she pulled from the counter. "Really?"

"Yeah."

"That's great. I'm happy for you."

"It is great. She's great. But what's up with you?"

Tears welled up in Charlotte's eyes and she shook her head. "I can't tell you. Not yet."

"Why not?"

"Because I haven't told Brian yet, and he deserves to know first."

Harry folded his arms across his chest. "Charlotte. I won't tell him. You obviously need to talk about it. What's going on?"

She huffed and dropped the dish towel onto the counter then covered her face with her hands. Finally she crossed her arms and took a deep breath, meeting Harry's eye. "I'm pregnant."

Harry's eyes went wide. "What? I thought you—"

"Had my tubes tied? Yeah. I did. *And* Brian had a vasectomy. I'm a walking statistic."

"Wow." If there was anyone in the world that could handle another baby, it was Charlotte. And Brian, too. They were great parents. But five kids? That sounded like a level of crazy Harry couldn't even imagine. "Five kids is a lot."

Charlotte whimpered. "I don't think I can do it, Harry. I'm so tired. This might kill me."

Harry moved across the kitchen and pulled his sister into a hug. "You could consider yourself a walking statistic, but you could also consider yourself a walking miracle. It's actually kind of amazing, isn't it? And maybe it'll be a little girl."

Charlotte sniffed and leaned into him. "A girl might be nice."

He rubbed his hands up and down her back. "You're going to be amazing. And you'll have lots of people to help. Brian, Mom and Neil, and now that I'm not such a mess, I can help too."

"I know. Logically, I know all of that. I'm just scared."

Harry reached around the counter and pulled a bar stool over to where Charlotte stood. "Here." He nudged the stool forward. "Sit. I'll finish the cinnamon rolls."

"Do you even know how?"

"I'm very good at following instructions. And it looks like you did the hardest part."

Charlotte walked him through the last few steps of rolling and cutting the dough. As he filled the greased sheet pans sitting behind him, Charlotte leaned her back against the counter, her hands resting in her lap.

"So you think Zoey will stick around then?"

Harry glanced up. "What do you mean?"

"Well, she lives in Chicago, right? She wasn't planning to stay here permanently."

"No, but, she has family here, and she seems to like it. I don't think it would be all that hard for her to transition."

"You haven't talked about it though?"

They *hadn't* talked about it. They'd inched around the subject a few times, but Harry got the sense Zoey didn't want to. It made him a little nervous, but things were so good between them. He didn't want to risk messing things up by demanding they talk about their future too soon. "It's only been a few weeks. We're just having fun. Getting to know each other."

"Do the kids know?"

Harry moved the last roll to the pan. "What's with the inquisition? Yes, the kids know. It's kind of hard to hide it because Zoey and I are almost never together when the kids aren't there. Our schedules don't really allow for traditional dating."

"Sorry. I don't mean to sound critical. Just consider this a gentle reminder. The divorce was hard on Hannah. She's with Zoey all day, and now she's seeing you and Zoey together. You guys might just be getting to know each other, but Hannah's probably already thinking Zoey's going to be her new mommy."

"That's not what Hannah thinks," Harry said, even as the expression he'd seen on Hannah's face just that morning flashed into his mind.

"Are you sure?" Charlotte asked emphatically.

Harry didn't answer. Hannah did love Zoey. She talked about her all the time when they weren't all together. But surely she understood—except, why would she understand? Hannah was only five. He couldn't expect her to understand the nuances of adult dating.

"I'm just saying. You probably ought to make sure your kids remember that Zoey's only staying for the summer. Then if she does go back to Chicago, she isn't breaking their hearts as well as yours."

Harry took a deep breath. "That's good advice."

"Also maybe tell Zoey she can't break your heart, okay? At least not until after this baby is born. It's my turn to be the needy one for a change. I won't be able to survive this without your help."

He wanted to think dating Zoey wouldn't end in a broken heart, even if she did end up leaving. He wasn't *that* invested. She could go back to Chicago at the end of the summer and they could part knowing they'd had a good time together and that was that. But even as he thought the words, he knew they weren't true. Zoey wasn't the kind of woman you only casually dated. She was the real deal. If they kept this up, he *would* fall for her. The thought was exhilarating, but it was also terrifying. He'd been crushed when Samantha had left him; he wasn't sure he could handle that kind of rejection again.

CHAPTER 9

ZOEY PULLED HARRY'S SUV into the parking lot and surveyed the park scene in front of her.

"I see Carlie!" Hannah said from the back seat behind her. "And Rowan!"

"Let's hurry then," Zoey said, unbuckling her seatbelt. "Can you help Oliver with his buckles?"

With a bag of snacks and another bag of toys and a spare change of clothes for Oliver—that kid was notorious for falling into mud puddles—strapped over her shoulder, Zoey led the children into the playground area. Hannah immediately darted off to find her friends. Zoey deposited all her gear at an empty bench in what she hoped to be neutral territory, then settled Oliver into the nearby sandbox with his dump truck and a shovel.

"Zoey!" one of the moms called as soon as she'd approached her empty bench. "There's room over here."

It would be rude to turn them down, wouldn't it? Zoey thought about faking a phone call but didn't think she was enough of an actress to pull it off. Besides, these were nice women. How bad could it truly be? Zoey grabbed her things and moved to the cluster of benches a half-dozen moms occupied. She was actually a little closer to Oliver from her new seat; at least that was a good thing.

"We've missed you the past few weeks," one mom said. Rebecca, maybe? Or was it just Becca?

"Oh. Thanks. Oliver was sick one week, and then I think we skipped because of the rain the week after that." It *had* been raining, Zoey remembered. Briefly. But Harry had finished shooting early that day and he'd surprised them just after lunch. They'd ended up spending the afternoon together. She'd take that over a semi-formal playdate any day.

"How have you been?" another woman with red hair asked. Zoey couldn't even pretend to remember her name. "How's the job?"

"Great. I'm enjoying the kids," Zoey answered.

"I'm sure the kids are so sweet. But how much do you see of their dad?"

"Rebecca, stop," the redhead said. "You're being nosy."

Zoey made a mental note. *Rebecca.*

"Oh, come on, Ashley," Rebecca said. "You know you're all dying to ask." She looked back to Zoey. "Is he as gorgeous in person as he is on television?"

"Um, haven't you all met him before? He's never brought the

kids to Park Play?"

"Never," Ashley said. "His sister brought them for a little while, but Harrison himself? He's pretty elusive."

"Do you know if he's dating anyone?" Rebecca asked.

"Oh my gosh," Ashley said. "Seriously? You've been divorced five minutes and you're hitting up Harrison Beckford's nanny for inside information?"

Rebecca rolled her eyes. "I'm just curious. He's *also* divorced, you might recall. I'm wondering if he's ready to start dating again."

Zoey just smiled. Maybe they didn't actually expect her to respond. They seemed pretty content talking about Harrison without any of her input.

"So?" Rebecca said, her attention back on Zoey. "Anything you can share?"

Zoey sighed. So much for *that* theory.

There was no way she was admitting to women she hardly knew that Harrison *was* dating someone and that the someone was her. They hadn't told anyone yet, outside of family, and while they hadn't talked about specifics, Zoey imagined the rules were different for someone like Harrison. Going public with a relationship was a decision. Almost an event. Particularly with him so fresh off of a divorce.

"I don't think it's my place to talk about Harrison's personal life."

"She told us that last time, didn't she?" Ashley said. She looked Zoey right in the eye. "I promise we aren't going to bully you into talking."

Zoey smiled, grateful to have at least one ally. "Thanks."

"Seriously though," Rebecca said. She leaned back and angled her face to the sun. "Can you imagine? Having *him* to wake up to every morning?"

Zoey forced herself not to smile. She could imagine. Well, almost. They weren't exactly waking up together, but she was in his kitchen every day while he drank his morning coffee and she kissed him goodbye on his way out the door. And the kisses they shared when the kids *weren't* around sent enough fire coursing through her that she could easily imagine what falling asleep and waking up in his arms would feel like. That had to count for something.

"And I bet his house is absolutely gorgeous," Rebecca went on.

"I can at least speak to that," Zoey said. "His house is gorgeous. Like a magazine. It took five years to complete because he built the entire thing himself."

"That's seriously so sexy," another mom said. "To build the whole thing by hand?" She sighed and shook her head.

"Come on. Just one thing," Rebecca said.

"She *did* tell you one thing." Ashley rolled her eyes then shot Zoey a sympathetic look.

"But that was about his house. Surely there's something more . . . personal. One thing and I'll leave you alone," Rebecca tried again.

Zoey tugged on her bottom lip, trying to think of something

benign enough to share. "Um, he has a golden doodle named Marigold. She's really sweet."

Rebecca looked like maybe she wasn't going to leave Zoey alone for such an unsatisfactory answer. Before she could push any further, Zoey stood up. "I think I need to check on Oliver."

She settled onto the side of the sandbox and leaned forward, helping as Oliver scooped sand into the back of his truck and then drove it to the other side of the box where he dumped it onto an already impressive pile. "That's good work you're doing, Ollie."

"I build like Daddy," Oliver said without looking up from his truck.

"Yeah, you sure do, buddy. Great job."

"Hey."

Zoey looked up to see Ashley, the redhead, standing beside the sand box, her hands on her hips.

"Hey," Zoey said.

Ashley looked across the playground, yelling for her kid to stop swinging on the monkey bars then sat down beside Zoey. "I'm sorry if Rebecca made you uncomfortable. She's normally not that bad. But she's kinda reeling after her divorce. She got hurt pretty bad."

"It's totally fine. I don't mind her asking. I just, it's not my place, you know?" Somewhere in the back of her mind, Zoey knew that if she *did* keep dating Harry, eventually the public would know. These women would know. And they'd likely figure out that she'd been dating him even while they asked her all their pointed questions. Still, Zoey couldn't bring herself to care. She found herself oddly defensive of her privacy, of Harry's privacy. Is this what it would always be like? Strangers feeling perfectly empowered to ask questions about their private life?

"I totally get it," Ashley said. "And respect you for it. My husband works in film. He's a producer. He's worked in the industry long enough for me to have learned how much gossip can ruin people. I think it's awesome that you don't want to talk."

"Oh. Thanks."

"Hey. Let me see your phone. I want to give you my number."

Zoey only hesitated a moment before pulling her phone out of her pocket. She liked Ashley. Trusted her, even. She pulled up her Contacts app and handed the phone over.

Ashley keyed in her name and number. "If you ever need a friend, don't hesitate to text me. My daughter Rowan is good friends with Hannah. I'm sure you have friends and a life outside of your job, so no pressure. I'm just letting you know. We're not all—" She motioned her head back toward where Rebecca sat. "Like that." She grinned and closed out Zoey's contacts. Then she froze, Zoey's phone in her hands. She looked up at Zoey, her eyes wide, then slowly handed the phone back. "I'm guessing you didn't want me to see that."

Zoey snatched the phone back and closed her eyes, heat flooding her face. A few nights before at Nana's, when Harry and the kids had come over for dinner, she had taken a selfie of her and Harry snuggled together on the couch. Zoey was smiling directly at the camera, but Harry was looking at her. His nose was pressed against her cheek—he'd just kissed her—and he was smiling, his eyes closed. He looked like he was savoring the moment and the photo had made Zoey's breath catch when she'd first seen it. When she showed it to Harry, he'd taken her phone, saving the photo as the background on her home screen. "Now you can remember fifty times a day how I feel about you," he'd said.

"Oh gosh," Zoey said. "I'm—"

"I won't say anything," Ashley said, cutting her off. "I swear. I totally get why you didn't want to tell anyone."

"It's still just so new," Zoey said. "And I don't even know if I'm—" She took a deep breath. "I live in Chicago. I'm just here helping out my grandmother for a few months and I needed part-time work. I'm not even sure I'm staying in California after the summer ends."

"Wow," Ashley said.

"Sorry." Zoey shook her head. "I don't even know why I told you all of that."

"No, it's okay. A new relationship is big. And probably the fact that it's Harrison Beckford makes it feel even bigger."

Zoey huffed a laugh. "Yeah."

"Like I said," Ashley said. She pushed herself to standing. "Even if you just need someone to talk to, I'm here. And I promise I'll be discreet."

Zoey nodded. "Thanks."

Later that evening, Harry walked Zoey out to her car. Or, his car, really. He'd been letting her drive it back and forth to Nana's every day. The kids were watching a movie inside, giving them ten minutes of alone time before Zoey had to leave to go and relieve Cassandra.

Harry leaned against the car, looping his thumbs through the belt loops of her jeans and pulling her close. She leaned up and kissed him, one hand lingering on the scruff that covered his jawline. "So, um, something happened at the park today."

He tensed under her hands. "Something bad?"

"Not really. I mean, the kids are fine. It didn't have anything to do with them. But you remember the picture you turned into my phone wallpaper a few nights ago?"

"That's a really good picture."

She smiled, despite her worry. "Yes. It is. But one of the moms at the park saw it."

"Ohhh," Harry said.

Zoey bit her lip. "She said she wasn't going to say anything. There's another mom, Rebecca, who, if she had seen it, you'd probably have TMZ parked out in your driveway right now. But Ashley, I don't think she's like that."

"Ashley," Harry repeated.

"Rowan's mom?" Zoey said. "Do you know her?"

He shook his head. "I don't think so. Charlotte might."

"I'm sorry. She asked for my phone so she could give me her number and I didn't even think—"

"Zoey," Harry said, cutting her off. "You don't need to apologize. I don't care that she saw the picture."

Zoey stilled. It's not that she thought he'd be mad, but he was famous. People cared when famous people dated other people. "Oh. I guess I just thought your people would need to know or something. Doesn't the public care if you're dating someone?"

"Sure they do. But that doesn't mean I have to care that they care. Let people speculate. Let them talk. I'm not obligated to provide information."

Of course he wasn't. Zoey knew that. But she'd never dated a celebrity before. She could only guess about what sorts of things his PR people needed to know about and what they didn't. "I guess that's good news then. I'll stop drafting a letter to the public in my head, detailing all the reasons why I'm qualified to date you."

Harry smiled, the resulting lines etched into his face nearly making Zoey swoon. "I could write a letter detailing why you're qualified, but I'm not sure it would be approved for general audiences."

"Harry!"

He chuckled, nuzzling his face into her neck. "I have to go to a thing in a couple of weeks."

Zoey leaned back so she could see his face. "A thing?"

"The network says I have to be there. It's a charity thing. Red carpet. Press. The whole deal."

Zoey nodded. "Okay."

"Come with me."

"What?"

"Come with me. Be my date. Officially. Then it won't matter

who sees our picture at the park."

Zoey's heart pounded in her chest. The idea of going some-where so public both thrilled and terrified her at the same time. "That sounds big."

"It doesn't have to be. People take dates to these things all the time."

"But you just got a divorce, Harry. A kind of public one. You showing up with a date is going to make people talk."

"The divorce was over a year ago. Let them talk. Let them see how happy you make me."

Zoey hesitated. "I don't know. I'd have to figure something out with Nana." That was only half of the reason she hesitated. Walking a red carpet as Harry's date meant that everyone, in-cluding her colleagues back in Chicago and worse, her mother, would know that she was dating Harrison Beckford. It likely wouldn't hurt her chances at landing an anchor position. News anchors were allowed to have personal lives. If anything, the extra media attention might only help her, not that she would ever intentionally leverage a relationship with Harry to benefit her own career.

But public commitment felt so much bigger than evenings at Nana's house chilling on the couch, or goodbye kisses after morning coffee. Was she ready for it? Was it what she wanted?

"I guess it's too much for your parents to fly in for the week-end?"

Zoey nearly balked at the thought. Her mother would *love* that she was dating Harrison Beckford. Not because he was a celebrity, though she'd love that part as well, but just because he was stable. Settled. Employed. With a house and a life Zoey could easily step into. Her mother was the last person she wanted to see right now.

"Or we could talk to Cassandra," Harry added, clearly sensing her hesitation. "I'm sure we could figure something out so you could be gone for one night. But no pressure," he quickly amended. "It's most important that you feel comfortable leaving her."

"No, I know. I'm sure we could figure something out. It wouldn't be a big deal for you to leave the kids?"

"Absolutely not. My mom can handle them. Or Charlotte, even."

Zoey shook her head. "Don't ask Charlotte. She doesn't need anything extra on her plate right now."

"Okay. Then my mom." The light in his eyes dimmed. "You're still hesitant to say yes."

Zoey had felt hesitant, but when she looked at the hope in Harry's eyes, she could hardly remember why. "No. Not hesitant. Let's do it. I want to come." Zoey smiled, allowing her enthusiasm to push away the fear still clinging to her heart. She wouldn't think about Rebecca at the park who would soon know *exactly* who Harry was dating, along with every other person who cared enough to look it up on the internet. She wouldn't think about her life back in Chicago, and the very pressing question of whether or not she'd be willing to walk away from that life to live this one instead.

She trusted Harry. She wanted a relationship with him. If that meant embracing the very public parts of his life, then so be it. She would figure everything else out later.

CHAPTER 10

Harry walked through the kitchen of the little coastal cottage his team had been gutting over the past week, his assistant, Jason, following close behind. It wasn't really a kitchen anymore. It was more an empty shell with some exposed plumbing. But by the end of the following afternoon, it would look like a kitchen again. Cabinets would be arriving within the hour, floors were going in first thing the next morning, and the appliances and fixtures would be in a few hours after that.

"What about the French doors?" Harry asked. "Will they be here in time?"

Jason nodded. "The truck has already left the warehouse. It'll be here by six."

"Perfect. And Tyson will be here early to finish the install before we start filming?"

Jason nodded again. "Yes, and yes."

"Good. I want to get shots of the floors in progress, but the door already needs to be in before that happens."

"Yep. It's all on the schedule for tomorrow." He pulled a file out of a portfolio and handed it to Harry. "Mary wants you to look these over. Notes on the next project. A young couple modernizing grandma's house to fit the needs of their growing family."

Harry flipped through the photos. "Looks like the house has good bones," he said. "Built when?"

"1923," Jason said quickly.

Harry smiled. Jason used to have to look for information like that when Harry asked. Lately, it seemed like he anticipated Harry's questions before he'd even had time to voice them.

Jason rolled his eyes, clearly having noticed Harry's glee. "What? Your questions are very predictable. Is it so surprising that I've figured you out?"

Harry handed the file back to Jason. "Tell Mary I approve."

"Friday or Monday for pre-reno walkthrough?"

Harry scratched the back of his neck and looked around the cottage. They'd probably finish up by Wednesday, which meant cleaning would happen Wednesday night. That meant staging, and post-renovation clean shots would happen on Thursday. They'd be wrapped by Thursday afternoon at the latest.

"If she's offering Monday as an option, let's go with that. I think everyone deserves a long weekend." Harry crossed through the living room and out the front door toward his truck.

"Got it," Jason said, making notes as he followed. "Okay,

last thing. The network called again, wanting to know if you're going to the charity event next Sunday night."

Harry unbuckled his tool belt and dropped it into the passenger seat of his truck.

"This is the fifth time that Beth Ann has called me to ask what your plans are."

"That many?"

Jason pulled out his buzzing phone. "Oh, look." He turned the screen to face Harry, revealing Beth Ann's name, then silenced the incoming call. "Now it's six times."

Harry smirked. "You really don't like talking to Beth Ann, do you?"

Jason scowled. "Don't pretend like you don't also think she's scary. You need to go to this thing, Harrison, and you need to bring a date. Your adoring public hasn't seen you looking happy in too long. Did you read Greta's email this morning? She explained all of this. It's time to leave the *recently divorced* label behind and let women swoon over you a little bit. The network needs you to do this; your personal branding needs you to do this."

Harry leaned against his truck. "You know how much I hate this part of the job." It wasn't that he hated getting dressed up, or even hated going to charity events. If it was a cause that resonated with him, he was happy to offer his image and his financial backing. He just hated the obligation. That so many people had a say in where he went and why he went there. "But even if I hadn't read Greta's email this morning, I'd still go to the event."

"Harry, you have to—" Jason paused. "Wait, what? You're going?"

Harry grinned. "I'm going, and I'm taking Zoey."

"Oh. Wow. Okay. That's great news. I'll let Beth Ann know. Do you, um, do you want me to talk to Greta about Zoey?"

Harry raised his eyebrows in question, then climbed into his truck, cranking the engine before lowering his window to finish the conversation with Jason. "Why do we need to talk to Greta about Zoey? She's coming with me. It'll make people talk, but that's nothing we aren't used to."

"Well, but, she's your nanny. That's likely to generate a little bit of extra attention. That you've started dating the help."

"No. That's not—don't say it that way." Harry ran a hand through his hair, suddenly frustrated by the turn the conversation had taken. "Zoey isn't the help. She's a family friend who agreed to temporarily help out with the kids."

"I don't know how Greta will spin that to the media. They're still going to call her your nanny. I mean, maybe not. But if anyone has seen her out and about with the kids, it won't take long for rumors to start. I'm not saying there's anything *wrong* with dating your nanny. But after the way they treated you during the divorce? I'm sure the tabloids will find a way to make it look scandalous."

Harry leaned his head back against the seat. "She's a news anchor from Chicago. She's got a master's degree. A career. Can we make sure *that's* the information that makes it to the press?

Sort of pre-empt the possibility of the nanny angle becoming the story?"

"So, leak information on purpose so people know who she is before the event?"

"Exactly."

"Good thinking. I'll talk to Greta. How does Zoey feel about all of this?"

Harry shrugged. "She's good with it. She wants to go." He tried not to think about the way she'd hesitated when he'd asked her to go with him. It had been nice keeping his relationship with Zoey quiet. The fact that they never went out, just bounced between his house and Emily's had made that easy so far. But if they kept dating—and he wanted them to—their world couldn't stay that small forever. People would eventually find out, if not at the charity event, then some other time. Admittedly, Zoey had a lot more on the line than he did. He'd grown used to living with minor celebrity status, to being recognized when he was out and about, to the constant interest and speculation regarding his personal life. But by agreeing to go, Zoey was sacrificing a measure of anonymity that she might not get back for a long time. That was plenty of reason for her to hesitate.

He could only hope she thought he was worth the risk.

CHAPTER 11

ZOEY STOOD BACK FROM the mirror at the end of the hallway and twisted to the side, looking at the buttons that cascaded down the back of her dress.

"You look perfect," Nana said from her chair in the living room. "Like you belong on the red carpet."

Zoey had to admit, the dress was perfect. Blue silk, asymmetrical with one shoulder strap and cascades of fabric cinching around her waist before falling in waves to the floor. The blue looked stunning with her dark hair, which she wore swept to the side to compliment the flow of the dress. She'd didn't think she'd ever looked so beautiful.

Zoey crossed the living room and sat down, but then stood back up again. Would sitting wrinkle her dress? She shook her hands, as if that alone would chase away her nerves, then wiped at the beads of sweat forming on her upper lip. "Ugh, I cannot start sweating!" She walked into the kitchen and opened the freezer, using the door to fan her face.

Cassandra came up behind her. "Here," she said, taking the freezer door from Zoey's hand. "Let me." She shifted Zoey into the space behind the freezer door, so the cool air pressed against the back of her neck, and picked up a thick magazine from the counter, using it to fan Zoey's face.

"Ohhh, that helps," Zoey said.

"You're going to do fine," Cassandra said. "This is Harry we're talking about. How long has it been now? A month? Six weeks? You don't have anything to be nervous about."

"Five weeks," Zoey said. "But I'm not nervous about Harry. I'm nervous about everyone else. What if they don't like me? What if they don't think I'm pretty enough to be dating *the* Harrison Beckford?"

Cassandra scoffed. "Since when did this become about being pretty enough for anyone? You are a strong, independent woman, and any man, famous or not, would be lucky to spend an evening in your company even if you wore a paper bag over your head. You have more to offer than your looks, sweetheart. Don't forget that."

"Amen," Nana shouted from the living room.

Zoey took a deep breath. She could do this. "Thank you for coming over," she said to Cassandra. The nurse wasn't technically on duty—she'd come over as a friend—which made Zoey all the more grateful that the woman had become a part of her grandmother's life. She was the real deal.

A knock sounded on the front door and Zoey's heart

lurched. "I'll get the door," Cassandra said. "You best get out of the freezer."

Zoey moved into the living room and grabbed her bag, then moved over to kiss Nana goodbye. Cassandra returned, Harry on her heels.

Zoey's breath caught in her throat. Harrison Beckford knew how to wear a suit. Dark gray, impeccably tailored, with a vest and a black tie, with the shoes and the hair and . . . Zoey swallowed. She needed to speak. "Hi," she finally managed.

Harry smiled. "You look beautiful."

"Thank you. So do you."

He held out his hand. "Shall we go?" They said goodbye to Nana and Cassandra then left through the front door. A sleek black limousine waited for them at the curb.

"Wow," Zoey said. "I guess you don't drive yourself to these things, do you?"

"Part of the perks," Harry said.

A driver waited for them, opening the door as they approached the car.

"After you," Harry said.

Zoey climbed into the limo and settled herself on the rear seat. Harry sat down beside her and reached out to squeeze her hand.

"Seriously, Zoe. You're stunning."

Zoey looked down at the blue silk she'd spent way too much money on. "Thanks. Any last-minute pointers? Red carpet dos and don'ts?"

"Jason will take your bag when we get out of the car and return it to you when we reach our seats. Other than that, just smile a lot and hold on to my hand."

Zoey nodded. "I'll be with you the entire time, right?"

"The whole time," Harry assured her. "There might be a reporter or two who want to ask a few questions, but mostly it will just be photos. If anyone asks who you are, I'll introduce you as my date, Zoey Williamson. That's it. It won't take long for people to try and figure out who you are, but Greta intentionally leaked info about you being a family friend and a news anchor in Chicago, which should be enough to keep them from digging too far into your personal life, though, if you have any public profiles you'd like to make private, it's probably a good idea to do that now."

Zoey's job already required that she have a pretty carefully curated online presence. She did have public profiles, but they were pretty basic. She never posted personal stuff. "I think I'm probably good on that front."

"I guess with your work you've already thought about that," Harry said.

"On a smaller scale, for sure, but yes." She closed her eyes and took a couple of cleansing breaths. "Geez, why am I so nervous?"

Harry chuckled. "Did you get this nervous before you went on the air back in Chicago?"

Her eyes popped open. "Never. But this is entirely different. People didn't watch the news to see *me*. They watched the news to get the news. But people are going to be taking pictures of *me*. Well, I mean, of you, really. But I'll be with you and that means they're all going to be speculating about who I am and what I'm doing with you and whether or not we're just dating or if we've fallen in love. I don't understand how you're so chill about this."

"Well I *was* feeling chill. If you keep this up, we're both going to be a mess by the time we get there." The laughter in his voice and the warmth in his eyes told Zoey not to take Harry seriously. "It's going to be fine," he said. "I promise. You're going to be the smartest, most talented, most beautiful woman in the room. Everyone is going to be amazed by you."

Zoey took another deep breath. "So, I'm not going to be introduced as your nanny?"

Harry raised their clasped hands to his lips and kissed the side of her wrist. "No. But I've never really thought of you as the nanny. Maybe for the first week, but then I was just so . . . I don't know. You've always felt like a lot more than that."

Warmth filled Zoey's chest. "I'm really happy, Harry."

He grinned. "Me too."

Moments later, the limo pulled to a stop and Harry gave her hand a final squeeze. "Are you ready to do this?"

They stepped out of the limousine into a sea of people, photographers calling Harry's name, yelling for his attention. Through it all, he was cool and calm, guiding her along the red carpet, pausing at intervals for different photographers to get their shots.

At one point, Harry pulled her close, an arm wrapped tightly around her waist and whispered into her ear. "This is so much easier with you beside me," he said.

The gesture only increased the flashes of the photographers' cameras. If they'd had any doubt about whether or not she and Harrison were a couple before, their doubts were likely gone now.

The rest of the evening passed in a blur. Zoey managed to keep it together when they were seated at a table with an actress she'd seen in a movie less than a week before and the lead singer from one of her favorite bands. The food was incredible, the dessert good enough she nearly asked the waif-like actress if she could eat hers as well, and the entertainment was better than she'd expected. The benefit was for a nonprofit organization focused on providing legal support and translation services to immigrant asylum seekers; by the end of the night, it was a cause she was happy to support both by her presence—she was sure Harry's network had paid prettily for their tickets—and with her own donation.

After drinks and more schmoozing and shaking hands with a dozen different people she was sure she'd never remember, she and Harry finally found themselves back in the limo.

Zoey collapsed back against the seat. "That was exhausting."

Harry loosened his tie. "Tell me about it. You were amazing though."

"I about lost it when John Krasinski and Emily Blunt stopped and said hello."

"John's a nice guy. We had dinner a few months back. You'd like him." Harry leaned against the seat but turned himself sideways, so he faced Zoey. "I don't want to take you home yet."

Zoey grinned. "I don't *want* to go home yet."

They wound up at a sleepy little basement jazz club they had to walk through an alley and descend a set of stairs to find. Had she been following directions on her own, without Harry to lead her, Zoey would have turned back three steps into the alley. But once they were inside the club, she was glad Harry had known where he was going. The club's atmosphere was nearly perfect. The place was full, but not crowded, the music just loud enough. Seated in a highbacked round booth in the corner, they could talk comfortably without having to shout over the music, but also without having to worry about anyone overhearing their conversation.

"This place is amazing," Zoey said.

"I used to come here all the time," Harry said. "Before the divorce."

Zoey traced her fingers over the folded napkin that sat on the table in front of her. "Things were different then," she said, a statement, not a question.

"Yeah. Really different."

"Were you as involved with the kids as you are now? Before the divorce?"

Harry frowned, his eyes dropping to the table.

Zoey slid a hand under the table and rested it on his knee, giving it a quick squeeze. "Hey. I'm sorry. I didn't mean for that to sound like judgment."

"It's okay," he said. "The truth hurts. Honestly, that was probably part of the problem. Samantha didn't want to be a mom, but maybe if I'd been around more, been more involved . . . I don't know. Entertainment news was not particularly kind to me during the divorce. Samantha made some pretty public accusations about me being an absentee dad, about her giving up her dreams so I could live mine. A lot of what they said was completely fabricated, but there was enough truth in the reporting to make me realize I had to change. The kids deserved better. And with their mom so completely checked out, I couldn't afford not to be all in."

"I love that about you," Zoey said. "Watching you be a dad? It's clear the kids are your top priority."

Harry shook his head. "It hasn't always been that way."

"You're doing a good job, Harry. Single parenting is hard."

A waiter showed up beside their table and took their drink order, before leaving them to their conversation.

"What about you?" Harry asked. "Do you want a family?"

Nerves skittered through Zoey's gut. It was a big question. A consequential question. She shrugged, trying to play off her nerves. "Yeah. I mean, I'm not looking to have a baby right now or anything, but, yes. It's always been a part of the plan."

Harry leaned forward, surprising her with a quick kiss. She leaned forward when he went to pull away, catching his face with her hand and pulling him back for a second and then a third kiss.

"I sometimes worry that my kids might scare women away," Harry said, his lips still close.

She kissed him one more time. "Your kids? Have you met your kids? They're nearly perfect."

"Yeah, but . . . the instant family. It isn't what a lot of women dream of."

Instant family. Funny. Zoey hadn't thought of it like that. She'd known about Harry's kids and realized they were a package deal. But she'd never thought of herself as anything other than the nanny. But if things kept up with Harry, that wouldn't always be the case. She wouldn't be a nanny. She'd be a *mom.*

She pushed her fears aside and focused on the man in front of her. "I think you're worth it, Harry. You don't have anything to worry about."

Harry hesitated and another pulse of fear snaked through Zoey's gut. He was hitting all the hard subjects tonight, wasn't he? "What about Chicago?" he finally said. "Has that always been a part of your plan?"

Zoey pulled away from Harry and pushed her fists into her lap. The implications of that question felt even bigger. "So I guess we're going to have this conversation now?" Even as she said the words, she wished she could call them back. She sounded defensive. Why was she defensive?

Harry reached for her hand. "We don't have to have this conversation now. Not if you don't want to."

Zoey kept her eyes down. She couldn't look at him. Couldn't see the warmth she knew filled his expression. "Harry—" she started, pausing when her voice cracked. Suddenly, her emotions made sense. She wasn't defensive, just *scared*. She finally looked up. "We can talk about it."

"I'm not going to pretend like I don't want you to stay in California, Zoe. But I see how quickly Ms. Emily is improving. She's not going to need you much longer, and I guess I'm wondering what that means. Do you want to go back to Chicago?"

It felt like a billion-dollar question.

She did want to go back. She couldn't just stay in California and be Harry's nanny. That wasn't a career; not for her, anyway. She'd been checking her email daily, hoping to hear back from Channel 4 about the anchor position. She wouldn't be that anxious to receive an answer if she didn't still want to be there. But she also couldn't begin to imagine walking away from her relationship with Harry. It was good. *So* good. Better than any relationship she'd ever had before, and she'd had some pretty good ones.

"I don't know what I want to do about Chicago," she said. "But I do know I don't want to leave you."

He smiled, but it wasn't a real one. Not really. It didn't come close to reaching his eyes. "There are news stations in Los Angeles," he said. "Lots of them."

There was a boyish hopefulness to his comment that warmed Zoey from the inside out. "That's true."

"Though, I suppose there are also homes that need remodeling in Chicago."

Zoey rolled her eyes. "Nice try. We both know that's about

the most impractical thing you could ever suggest. Your show is here. Your parents. Your house. Your kids' lives. Your sister and her family. You can't leave California."

He sighed. "I know. But I'm crazy enough about you, you might convince me to do it anyway."

Zoey leaned in and kissed Harry again, her hand reaching up to cradle the back of his head. "Let's not think about it right now," she finally whispered. "For now, I'm not going anywhere." It was a cop-out answer and she knew it. But what else was she supposed to say? She couldn't tell him how she felt about Chicago because she didn't actually know. It felt like she was living in a parallel universe. This was her California life. Her living with Nana, dating Harrison Beckford, hanging out with two amazing kids life. But her Chicago life still existed. Her news anchor life. Her independent career woman life. The problem was that no matter the mental gymnastics she tried to perform, she couldn't seem to make the two lives intertwine. It was like they existed on completely different planes. She just couldn't explain all that to Harry. Especially not tonight.

Harry pulled back, catching her eye. He held her gaze a long moment, his expression radiating sincerity and warmth. "I'm falling in love with you, Zoey," he said, his tone gentle.

Zoey closed her eyes, chills racing up her spine and out to every fingertip. She had imagined what hearing those words would feel like. She was falling for him, too. She knew she was. But the thought of admitting as much made fear grip her midsection, constricting her lungs until she worried she might stop breathing. To say the words back felt big. Consequential. Only made worse by the pulsing neon sign in the back of her brain that said *Chicago, Chicago, Chicago.*

Since she couldn't answer Harry with words, she leaned forward and answered him with another kiss. She didn't hold back, willing all of the words she was too afraid to say into the gesture. She tilted her head and parted her lips, deepening the kiss. Harry pulled her closer, accepting her, welcoming her. Somehow, he grounded her and lifted her into the atmosphere all at the same time. She felt safe, anchored, like she was exactly where she needed to be, but also felt as though she could fly around the room with the energy coursing through her. It was intoxicating.

She wasn't able to give Harry the reassurance he wanted. Not yet. Hopefully for now, that kiss would be enough.

Harry dropped Zoey off just after two in the morning. She sank onto the couch in Nana's living room, wishing it wasn't so late. She needed wisdom. Answers. Clarity. But then, even if it wasn't a ridiculous time of night, she didn't know who she would call.

Earlier that night, she'd ignored a text from her mother. *ZOEY WHY DIDN'T YOU TELL ME CALL ME IMMEDIATELY.*

For her mother to leave out punctuation of her texts was very telling. She'd probably been on the phone all evening with her sisters and cousins and neighbors and old high school friends and anyone else she could think to tell. Before long, she'd be researching wedding dress boutiques in Southern California and pricing out designer invitations. She probably already had three different "mother of the bride" dresses in her online Stein Mart cart. No, she couldn't call her mother. Hers was not the advice Zoey needed.

Nana was usually the voice of reason in Zoey's life, but in this instance, she wouldn't be much better than Mom. Besides, Nana loved Harry. She'd never be able to filter out how much and how long she'd cared about him to give Zoey unbiased advice.

Zoey didn't even have a friend she felt like she could call. She was running kind of low in that category as of late; her crazy work schedule had all but ruined the few friendships that had survived grad school. Morning news anchors got up when most people were going to bed which meant she'd mostly slept through Chicago's active night life the past few years. The people she *had* hung out with in Chicago had all been coworkers. A few of them would be willing to listen, Veronica would for sure, and would try to offer advice, but they didn't know her well enough to know what she needed.

Ashley from the park had offered to listen, but she knew Zoey least of all.

A wave of loneliness pulsed over Zoey, and oddly made her wish she could curl up in Harry's arms and forget about everything. But that was the least practical impulse of all. She'd never make a reasonable decision about what to do about Harry if *Harry* himself was in the room.

Her heart said she wanted him. But it couldn't be that simple, could it?

"Hey."

Zoey looked up to find Cassandra leaning against the kitchen door jamb. "Hey. I didn't think you were awake."

"I was just having some tea. Emily woke up with a pretty bad headache and it took a while for her to settle back to sleep."

Zoey tensed. "Is she okay? What caused the headache?"

"Calm down," Cassandra said. "It's nothing to worry about. Everybody gets a headache every once in a while. You look like *you* could use some tea. Want to join me?"

Zoey nodded and stood up, dropping her heels onto the couch before following Cassandra into the kitchen.

"How was the night?" Cassandra asked.

Zoey pulled up the skirt of her dress and sank into a kitchen chair. "Amazing. Magical. I met Jim from *The Office*."

"Fun. But I'm guessing that isn't what made the night magical." Cassandra set a mug of tea in front of Zoey then nudged the honey toward her. "What was it like to be on the arm of *the* Harrison Beckford?"

Zoey smiled. "He's pretty spectacular."

Cassandra's eyes narrowed. "And yet, you were still sitting there staring at your phone like someone just called to say your dog died. Why don't I believe you had a good time?"

"That's not it. I had an amazing time. It's just . . . I don't know if I can even explain it."

"Try me," Cassandra said.

Zoey heaved a sigh. "I felt myself . . . getting swept up, you know? It was intoxicating. The attention. The glamour. Having this incredibly gorgeous man that America is in love with put his arm around *me*. It made me feel important and . . . special, I guess."

"That hardly sounds like something to complain about," Cassandra said.

"No, I know. I'm not complaining. But it also made me miss my job."

Cassandra's brows furrowed. "How do you mean?"

"Tonight I was important because I was Harry's date. But when I'm working I'm important because I'm me. Because I have something to offer. I guess there's a part of me that's afraid that if I date someone whose life is as big as his, my life might . . . disappear."

It was the first time Zoey had actually voiced the fear out loud, but the truth of it resonated in her gut in a profound way.

"That's not how he sees you though, is it?" Cassandra asked. "I've been around enough to see the way he looks at you. It isn't like you're an ornament on his arm."

"I know. He's never made me feel that way. He even had his publicist make sure that if people try to find out who I am, the information they'll find will include stuff about my career. But if we're going to be together, I'm going to have to move to California. That feels like a really big deal. I don't know if I'm ready for it. And I think I'm maybe afraid that all the glitz and glamour and money will influence me without me realizing it's happening. But that shouldn't be what the relationship is about."

"Now, wait a minute," Cassandra said. "You've been on *one* glamorous date with the man. Most of the time, you're hanging out with his kids, or your grandma. There's nothing glamorous about that."

"I know. But there's still a polish to his life. Money does that. The house is perfect. The kids have closets full of adorable clothes and matching shoes and monogrammed towels. The cars all have leather interiors. There's someone to clean the house and someone else to mow the lawn. And someone to watch the children, which, admittedly is a little weird since I'm the someone. But you know what I mean? It feels special being a part of a life like that."

"But Zoey, Harrison didn't grow up with all those things, did he? I've heard Emily talk about his humble beginnings. A man can have things without being defined by those things."

"That's true," Zoey said. "But it still doesn't fix the whole 'my life is in Chicago' problem."

"How do you feel about *him*?" Cassandra asked. "If you set all that other stuff aside. The stuff about your career and his career and his money. When you just think about the man, what do you feel?"

That was a question that hardly required any thought at all. "I think I might love him," Zoey said softly. "Is that crazy?"

"It's not crazy," Cassandra said. "And that's the feeling you need to trust the most. Everything else will work itself out in time."

CHAPTER 12

HARRY WAS STILL IN bed on Monday morning when he heard Zoey let herself in the front door. The patter of little feet running across the floor quickly followed, then the sound of Oliver's sleepy morning voice.

"Zoey," Oliver said.

"Hey, Ollie," Harry heard Zoey say. "Are you the only one up?"

She sounded as tired as Harry felt. He should have told her to take the morning off. He'd barely managed four hours of sleep himself. She couldn't have gotten much more than that. He glanced at his phone. Maybe it wasn't too late. He could text Charlotte and see if the kids could hang with her for a couple of hours—at least long enough for Zoey to take a nap.

He had to be on site for a pre-renovation walkthrough by ten. There wasn't anything he could do about his own exhaustion, but there was no reason for Zoey to be miserable as well. Before he could finish tapping out a text to his sister, Charlotte texted *him*.

MORNING SICKNESS SUCKS. Please send help. And ginger ale.

Harry frowned. Guess he probably *shouldn't* ask her to watch his kids for a few hours. He keyed out a response. *So sorry. I'm filming today. I'll send ginger ale though. Need anything else?*

He could probably have Jason swing by and drop a few things off, though Charlotte would probably hate having him just show up. Grocery delivery, maybe?

Brian out of town again? he texted. Charlotte's husband was unfailingly supportive, but he traveled for work quite a bit. Charlotte always texted her brother more when her husband was gone.

Just 'til tomorrow, she responded. *Ginger ale and Goldfish. And beef flavored ramen. And chicken nuggets for the kids.*

Got it, Harry texted back. *I'll have some things sent over.*

He quickly keyed out a text to Jason, asking him to get the groceries ordered and delivered. Technically, Charlotte could have ordered the groceries herself; there were delivery services everywhere. But he suspected she mostly just needed someone to care. After sending Jason the list, padded with a few additional things he thought Charlotte's kids might like, he ordered her a blueberry smoothie from the smoothie place closest to her house and paid a little extra for it to be delivered ASAP. Charlotte may think all she needed was ramen and ginger ale, but she'd probably benefit from something nutritious.

He was sitting on the edge of his bed, just finishing up the order when Oliver blasted into his bedroom and launched himself onto Harry's lap.

"Daddy awake!" Oliver said. His voice had lost the sleepy tone of a few minutes before and was full of energy and enthusiasm. If only it were that easy for adults.

Harry swung his son around and plopped him onto the bed before tickling him in all the places Oliver loved. "Where do you get all this energy, huh?" he asked, mussing Oliver's hair. "I wish you could give me some."

"Maybe this will help," Zoey said.

Harry looked up. She stood in the doorway of his bedroom, a mug of coffee in her hand. Even after only four hours of sleep, she looked rested and beautiful. Her hair was pulled back into a ponytail, and her face was bare, different than the glamorous look she'd worn the night before. But she was no less stunning.

She crossed the room and handed him the mug, her eyes roving over his bare chest and shoulders. "I tried to keep him busy hoping you were still sleeping, but once he realized you were awake, there was no keeping him from you."

Harry ran a hand across his face. "That's okay. I've been up a little while." He took a sip of the coffee then placed it on the small table beside his bed. "How are you? Exhausted?"

She offered a small smile. "Not too bad."

He reached for her from where he sat on the edge of the bed, curling an arm around her waist and pulling her close. At the same time, Oliver climbed onto his back, nuzzling his face into

Harry's neck, and reached a tiny hand out, curling it over Zoey's shoulder to loop them in an awkward three-way hug.

Warmth bloomed in Harry's chest. He'd missed feeling like a family. Feeling complete.

Hannah stumbled in a few minutes later. "Why are we all hanging out in here?" she asked, climbing onto the bed.

"Because your Dad was out super late last night," Zoey said. "But now he's got to get ready for work which means we need to go get some breakfast."

She scooped Oliver into her arms and reached for Hannah's hand. "Are you hungry?"

Hannah hardly looked Harry's way before taking Zoey's hand and following her to the kitchen. Contentment settled over him. His kids really did love Zoey.

Charlotte's warning from a few weeks before pinged in his mind. It would likely devastate the kids if Zoey decided to go back to Chicago. Even though it had only been a month and a half, she was fully integrated into their lives. The kids trusted her, relied on her. Once the week before, Oliver had fallen and bumped his head and ran to Zoey instead of Harry for comfort. She'd said she wasn't going anywhere the night before, and he trusted her. But for how long? That she didn't want to talk about Chicago made him nervous, yet he wasn't sure he wanted to push her. If he pushed too hard, would it do the opposite of what he wanted and push her away?

Still, Charlotte had been right. He had to think about his kids' feelings. What was best for them? It was so much more complicated than just what he wanted.

After showering and getting ready, he found Zoey and the kids in the kitchen. He moved to the sink and rinsed out his coffee mug. "What do you guys have planned for the day?" he asked.

"I want to go see Spencer," Hannah said from her place at the table. She scooped up a big bite of cereal. "Can we, Zoey? Can we go see Spencer?"

Zoey looked at Harry, an eyebrow raised. "Would Charlotte care?"

Spencer was Charlotte's second oldest and was one of Hannah's closest friends. She'd likely been missing hanging out with her cousin.

"Actually, she might appreciate a visit today. She texted this morning and she's feeling really terrible. Morning sickness. And Brian's out of town and I don't know. She seemed pretty low. It'd probably be nice for her to have someone else around to help with the kids."

Zoey didn't respond right away, and Harry wondered if he'd overstepped by asking. Was it too familiar of a thing for her to do? They'd hung out with Charlotte a few times, and it seemed like the women got along, but tripling the number of children in Zoey's care was a big ask.

"Are you asking like a boyfriend, wanting his girlfriend to help out his pregnant sister? Or are you asking as an employer who needs his nanny to watch his nephews for the day?"

Harry grinned. She'd said boyfriend.

"What?" Zoey said, mirroring his smile. "Why are you smiling?"

"Because you said boyfriend."

She pursed her lips and folded her arms. "I did, didn't I?"

Harry stepped close to her and rested his hands on her hips. He leaned in and kissed her quickly, not wanting to linger with the kids just behind them. "I would never pressure you into watching four extra kids all day as my girlfriend or as my nanny. I won't be mad if you want to chill here all day and relax. Especially after how little sleep you got last night."

"But?"

"No buts. Genuinely. I already had Jason order Charlotte some groceries, and I had a green smoothie delivered to her house for breakfast. I honestly wouldn't have even thought about you going over there had Hannah not mentioned Spencer."

Zoey nodded. "You're a good brother. You know that, right?"

Harry lifted one shoulder into a shrug. It had been too many years since he'd had the bandwidth or the appropriate perspective to be as good a sibling to Charlotte as she had been to him. "Just making up for lost time," he said.

CHAPTER 13

JUST BEFORE LUNCH, ZOEY ended up going over to Charlotte's after all. Not because she felt any sort of pressure from Harry to go, but because Hannah had been particularly clingy all morning. Playing with her cousins might give Zoey a little bit of a break. She'd thought about texting Ashley to see if Rowan was available to play, but she wasn't sure she was quite ready to face Harrison Beckford's adoring public so soon after their appearance at the charity event. Ashley had been cool, but a picture of Harrison and Zoey had already been featured on multiple entertainment news sites that morning. It just felt safer sticking to family members who already knew the ins and outs of their relationship.

Charlotte's oldest son let Zoey and the kids in. "Mom's in her bedroom," he said. He pointed down the hall. "That way."

Zoey put Oliver in the living room where the Disney Channel was showing reruns of his favorite cartoon. After asking the other kids to keep an eye on him, she went to find Charlotte.

"Charlotte?" Zoey called from the bedroom door.

Charlotte appeared in the bathroom doorway, a rag pressed to her face. Dark circles lined her eyes and strands of damp hair clung to her forehead.

"Hey," Zoey said, compassion filling her voice. "That bad, huh?"

Charlotte collapsed onto her bed. "I've seriously thrown up so many times in the past week. It's the worst. I'm so hungry, but nothing sounds good."

"Harry told me you weren't feeling good. I'm going to stay a few hours if that's okay. I'll feed the kids. Get them outside for a little bit. Is there anything else I can do for you?"

Charlotte shook her head. "Even just that is amazing. Thanks for coming over."

"It's not a big deal. Hannah's been missing Spencer anyway."

Charlotte smiled. "Those two are the cutest. They've been like that since they were tiny."

Zoey picked up Charlotte's water bottle from her nightstand. "Can I refill this for you?"

"Yes, please."

After a quick trip to the kitchen, with a slight detour through the living room to check on Oliver, Zoey took the filled bottle back to Charlotte. She paused in the doorway when her phone beeped with an incoming message. She pulled it out of her back pocket and froze.

The message was an email from Channel 4 in Chicago. They

liked the clips she'd sent in. And they wanted her to come in for an interview as soon as possible. She forced a breath in through her nose and out through her mouth. She didn't have to respond right away. It's not like they'd given her a specific day they wanted to see her. They'd just said as soon as possible. That could mean within a week, even two weeks, couldn't it?

She pushed the worry from her mind. She for sure couldn't figure things out while she was hanging out with Harry's sister.

"I saw the pictures," Charlotte said as Zoey set the water bottle down. "From last night. You guys make a cute couple."

"Thanks." She sat on the edge of Charlotte's bed. "I've been afraid to look at them."

"I bet. I'm sure it's overwhelming to see yourself all over national entertainment news. But from what I've seen, it's all complimentary. A lot of stuff about people being happy to see Harry dating again. Speculation about how long you've been together, whether or not there are wedding bells in your future."

"Oh, geez. That might be a little premature."

Charlotte smiled. "I don't know. Harry tends to fall hard and fast into everything he does. It might not be as far off as you think."

Zoey looked at her hands, squeezing them into fists in her lap. How was she supposed to respond to that?

"Can I be honest for a sec?" Charlotte asked.

Zoey looked up and met her eyes. "Of course."

"He really likes you, Zoey."

Zoey bit her lip. He loved her, even. He'd nearly told her as much the night before.

"He hasn't dated that much since the divorce. Definitely not anything serious. But it seems like things are different with you. He's different. I know you didn't come to California planning to stay. And that's totally your thing. I'm just worried about his kids. I don't want Harry to get hurt, but I worry more about Hannah and Oliver. The more they spend time with you and the more they see you and Harry together, the harder it's going to be for them to understand what's going on."

Zoey shook her head. "I know that. I'm not trying—"

"I've mentioned this to Harry, too," Charlotte said, cutting her off. "I know he doesn't want to pressure you because he doesn't want to push you away. But you can't string him along, Zoey. If you aren't planning on sticking around? He deserves to know."

Zoey tensed, trying to fight the defensiveness rising inside her. It's not like she'd been dating Harry for months and months. It had been *weeks*.

"It feels really early in our relationship for me to feel that kind of pressure," Zoey finally said, happy that her voice sounded so steady. "I'm not stringing him along. It hasn't even been two months."

"I know," Charlotte said. "It isn't really fair. But it is what it is, and it's definitely more complicated because the kids are involved and because you never intended to be here full time. If it were me making the decisions, I wouldn't have told the kids the two of you were dating. Just to make it easier on them should you decide to leave."

Zoey sighed. "I had that thought. But Harry seemed so sure. So much of the time we spend together is *with* the kids. He didn't want to have to pretend."

"I get that. Harry also tends to give everyone and every situation the benefit of the doubt without always thinking through the consequences. Plus, when he finds something or someone that he's passionate about, he's all in. I'm sure he's mostly thinking about the future you guys could have once you decide to stay."

"You mean, if I decide to stay."

"That's just it," Charlotte said. "You're saying if. I'm saying if. My hunch is that Harry is saying when."

"We haven't had the conversation though."

"Which means you haven't told him you're leaving, but you also haven't told him you're staying. Like I said. He's an eternal optimist. Prone to giving everyone the benefit of the doubt."

Zoey stifled a frustrated laugh. "Does the man not have any flaws? Any walls that he hides behind?"

Charlotte tilted her head thoughtfully. "He's pretty transparent. Granted, he made some stupid decisions when he first got famous. And his priorities were all kinds of messed up. But he's been so much better the past year or so."

"Yeah. He's told me about that a little. About how much he's changed."

"Zoey, look. I don't want to pressure you into making a decision right now. Just, be careful, okay? Think about the kids, too. And maybe talk to Harry about your decision. If you guys are a couple, you should make it together, right?"

Zoey did think about the kids. And about Harry. And about how much she didn't want to lose them. But she still couldn't bring herself to tell Channel 4 she wasn't interested. It felt so final. So . . . life changing. There would be other jobs. And Harry was right that she could always try and find a job in Los Angeles. But she'd worked so hard to establish herself in Chicago. And the Channel 4 job was *the* job she'd been thinking about for years. Starting over felt huge.

For three days she stared at the email, unable to respond.

Harry noticed she was distracted.

Nana noticed she was distracted.

Even Hannah asked her why she was always staring into space and not talking.

Zoey hardly knew how to answer. She was paralyzed. Overwhelmed. Terrified of making the wrong decision.

On Thursday morning, she took the kids to Park Play, deciding they needed the entertainment—she'd hardly been on her A-game the past few days—and since she'd have to face the mommy brigade eventually, she might as well go ahead and get it over with.

It took less than five minutes for Rebecca to descend upon her, ushering her into the circle of moms sitting next to the sandbox.

"Okay," Rebecca said. "Tell us everything. You've *obviously* been keeping some secrets."

"Lay off," Ashley said, immediately coming to Zoey's defense. "Can you blame her? We circled like vultures the first time we met her."

"Vultures is maybe a little harsh," Rebecca said. "Come on. Spill it. You were gorgeous, by the way. Loved the dress. But why didn't you tell us? How long have you been dating?"

Zoey forced a smile. "I, um, it's complicated."

"But you are dating, right?" Rebecca said.

"I thought that was pretty obvious after all the pictures and everything," Zoey said.

Rebecca closed her eyes. "Seriously. I'm so jealous. So tell us how it happened. And also, how does a news anchor from Chicago end up working as a nanny in California? I've been trying to figure that part out for days."

At least that was a question Zoey could answer. "I'm here taking care of my grandmother. She's recovering from a stroke and she needed someone to be with her in the evenings and on the weekends. I'm between jobs, so nannying felt like an easy thing to do to cover my expenses while I'm here."

"Right. So you just casually looked for a nannying job and started working for Harrison Beckford?"

"He's a friend of my grandmother's," Zoey explained. "I wasn't *looking* for a nannying job."

"Do you think you'll go back to Chicago?" Ashley asked. The gravity in her voice told Zoey she didn't ask the question lightly or just out of curiosity. Zoey sensed Ashley understood the multilayered nature of the question.

Before she could respond, Rebecca scoffed. "Are you kidding? Why would she leave now? She's dating Harrison *freaking* Beckford."

Ashley rolled her eyes. "Because her life is in Chicago. Her career is there."

"But she could move her career," another woman said, this one someone Zoey had never spoken to before. "Better yet, just give it up. She's with Harrison now. That's all I'd need if it were me."

"No joke," Rebecca said. "Plus, there are already two kids to take care of. That's basically a full-time career as it is. Why work if she doesn't have to?" Rebecca suddenly stood up, yelling across the playground as she ran after a little girl Zoey could only assume was her kid.

Zoey looked back at Ashley, fighting the panic rising in her throat. She'd been battling her fears since her conversation with Charlotte earlier that week. But Rebecca's comments seemed to ratchet everything up a notch.

"Hey, Harrison could afford another nanny," Ashley said calmly. "It's not like if you keep dating him you have to be an insta-mom."

But she would be, wouldn't she? She didn't need a degree in psychology to recognize that she'd filled a hole in Hannah's life by being with her every day. The last few days, they'd spent hours talking about kindergarten coming up in a couple of weeks. About all the things Hannah was afraid of, all the things she was excited about. They'd talked about first-day-of-school outfits and whether or not she wanted her dad to walk her all the way into her classroom or just drop her off at the door of the school like all of the bigger kids.

Hannah had even called her from Harry's phone before bed the night before so she and Oliver could say goodnight to her before they went to sleep.

It was too late to backpedal now.

Zoey had always dreamed of having a family. But in her head, it had always been something she would build slowly. She'd meet the guy. Fall in love with the guy. Marry the guy. Build the career. Buy the house. *Then* have a baby. When she felt ready. Jumping into a ready-made family with both feet, especially when her entire Chicago life was on the line was a big ask, even if the asker was the famous Harrison Beckford.

"Well, speak of the devil," Rebecca said, lowering her sunglasses and staring at something over Zoey's shoulder.

Zoey turned and saw Harry climbing out of his truck. She quickly stood and crossed the playground to meet him.

"Hey," he said as she approached.

She stopped in front of him. "Hi. What are you doing here?"

"I finished early. I thought we could take the kids somewhere together. To the zoo, maybe." He looked over her shoulder. "Would it help or hurt your situation if I kissed you hello?"

Zoey shrugged. "What if you just kiss me hello because I want you to?"

He grinned. "That is a good enough reason." He leaned down, his hand lingering on the small of her back while his lips pressed against hers. The intensity of the kiss caught Zoey by surprise. It wasn't a hello peck; it was more of a steamy, *hey baby* kind of kiss. Zoey was pretty sure more than one of the moms behind her gasped out loud.

Zoey pulled away, a shocked expression on her face. "You did that on purpose," she said playfully.

Harry shrugged, his grin wide on his face. "Maybe."

She smacked him on the chest. "There are children at this park, Mr. Beckford. I expect better behavior out of you."

He only laughed. "I'll get the kids, you get your stuff?"

"Uh-uh," Zoey said, taking his hand. "You're coming over and saying hello. After that public display, I'm not facing them by myself."

She tugged Harry toward the group of moms. She reached down and gathered up her stuff before tossing out a brief introduction. "Everyone, this is Harrison Beckford. Harry, this is everyone."

Harry shifted into performance mode—something Zoey still found fascinating—and greeted the women. He smiled for pictures, said hello to babies, and even offered a sincere opinion when one of the women asked him a remodeling question about her house. He was charming—*so charming*—an observation that filled Zoey with an emotion she hadn't expected.

She was jealous.

But jealous of who? His fans? The public? This wasn't the first time she'd seen him in *Harrison Beckford* mode. But the red carpet had felt different. The photographers and reporters had felt a little more removed, and he'd had his hand wrapped tightly around hers the entire night. But now, watching the moms fawn over her boyfriend, finding reasons to touch his arm or his shoulder, she realized how weird it was knowing that all the time, women all over the country were likely having entire conversations about how sexy he was, about how great it would be to meet him.

On the one hand, it was thrilling. He was *hers,* after all. And Charlotte had been right when she'd called Harry transparent. She didn't doubt his feelings for her at all. But on the other hand, would they ever be able to go anywhere when his fame wasn't competing for his attention? How would that play into regular life? Would they even be able to *have* a regular life?

Harry pulled a baseball cap onto his head and wore dark sunglasses when they took the kids to the zoo, but it still didn't completely curb the attention from strangers. At one point, while they stood outside the gorilla habitat, she noticed three different people standing off to the side, taking pictures of him.

Zoey stepped up beside him, slipping her hand into his. "Do you ever get used to that?" she whispered, motioning with her head toward the would-be paparazzi.

He squeezed her fingers briefly before dropping her hand so he could pick Oliver up. He shrugged. "You learn to ignore it." He pointed into the habitat. "Look, Ollie, do you see the baby gorilla? Right there with her mom?"

He made ignoring it seem easy, but the entire day left Zoey feeling shaken. She'd worried she'd be wooed by the glamour in

Harry's life. And thinking about the benefit and the red-carpet attention, she couldn't deny that was still a real possibility. But now she'd been forced to think about the downside to his fame, to experience it firsthand. It only made her more confused.

That evening after dinner, Zoey got a follow-up email from Channel 4. *Hi, Zoey. Just checking to make sure you got our email. We'd love to meet with you. Next Wednesday? Let me know ASAP.* The email was signed by the producer she'd worked with a few years prior.

Now she really did have to make a choice. She found Nana in the kitchen, wiping down the counters. A month ago, Zoey never would have let Nana stay on her feet long enough to do the simple task. But she'd made so much progress. Her walking was steady, her hand-eye coordination was so much better, and her speech was back to normal.

Zoey sat down at the kitchen table, setting her phone face down in front of her.

Nana turned around. "Hey. What's got you looking so glum?"

"I talked to Cassandra this afternoon before she left."

Nana dropped into the chair across from her. "Okay."

"She said your insurance is only paying for one more week of home-care?"

Nana nodded. "That's right. After that, I'm on my own."

"How do you feel about that?"

"Oh, I'm more concerned about being lonely than anything else. Cassandra has spoiled me with her easy company. But I feel fit as a fiddle these days. It's time for her to move on and help someone else."

Zoey bit her bottom lip, hesitant to meet her grandmother's eye. "What about me?"

Nana raised an eyebrow. "Are you ready to move on too?"

"I don't know." Zoey's shoulders fell. "I don't want to leave you. I love being here, and . . ."

"And Harry is here."

"Yeah." Zoey sighed. "Harry is here."

"But?" Nana prompted. "I can tell you're working up to tell me something. Just spit it out."

"Channel 4 in Chicago wants me to come in for an interview," Zoey said. She looked up. "Next Wednesday."

"Is that a big deal?"

"The biggest. It's the job I've wanted since I first started working. It's only an interview. They might have me guest anchor a night or two to see how I test with viewers. I don't have to go though. Not if you aren't ready to be on your own."

Nana rolled her eyes, a sight that nearly made Zoey giggle. For a split second, Nana looked fifty years younger, her sassy younger self shining through the wrinkles. "Don't even begin to pretend like I'm the reason you aren't sure if you should go. I'm fine, Zoey. You've seen that the last two weeks. We always knew you staying with me was temporary. Besides, your mother is coming in next week. Has she not told you that? She'll be here through Thursday so you can go to your interview no problem, supposing you work something out for Hannah and Oliver."

"Mom is coming here?"

Nana nodded. "Sunday night. Why didn't she tell you, I wonder?"

Zoey had been ignoring her mother since the benefit when photos of her and Harrison had hit the internet. She'd finally responded to her text with something vague and equally brief and then declined the dozen or so call attempts she had made. "She probably knew I'd find a reason to disappear if she did."

Nana frowned. "You've always gotten along with your mother. Why are you ignoring her now?"

Zoey sighed. She hadn't been fair to her mom and she knew it, but it still stung to have Nana call her out. "She hasn't done anything wrong. I guess I'm just feeling like I'm at a crossroads right now, and her advice is not the kind of advice I need. I don't think she likes that I'm working. You know how she feels, Nana. She wants me to have what she had. And *now* there's an actual man in my life and she's determined to make sure I get my hooks all the way in. That way, I can quit my job and let Harrison take care of me just like Dad did her."

"Zoey," Nana said, censure in her tone. "That's a bit harsh. Your mother was a good mother to you. There's nothing wrong with choosing to stay at home to raise your children. She gave you everything for years. That's no small sacrifice. She just doesn't want you to miss out on what brought her the most joy."

"I don't want to miss out on it either. But why can't I have a career too? Why does it have to be one or the other?"

"Has your mother ever said that to you? That it has to be one or the other?"

Zoey huffed. "No, but I can tell that's what she thinks."

Nana shook her head. "I don't think you give her enough credit, Zoey. She's proud of you. She wants you to get married; of course she does. Because she wants you to be happy. And her family is what made her the happiest. You can't hold that against her."

Nana was probably right. But there were too many things her mother had said over the years, too much history for Zoey to forget. Her mother would never value Zoey's career as much as Zoey did.

"I get it. I'm sorry. I love that Mom was with us when we were kids. I've always thought I would do the same thing someday. But she doesn't understand why my career is also important, maybe even more important right now."

"More important than what? Are we talking about relationships in general, or are we talking about one man, specifically?"

Zoey's shoulders fell. "Of course we're talking about Harry. I can't stop thinking about him."

"I thought that's what this conversation was about," Nana said. She reached across the table and took Zoey's hand, giving it a quick squeeze.

"Honestly, I don't even know if I *can* talk about it anymore. I've thought myself in circles all week long. But now the station has emailed again and needs me to confirm an interview ASAP and I think I have to do it. Even if I end up turning down the job and staying in L.A., I think I have to at least go and see how I feel about it."

"Have you told Harry?"

Zoey shook her head. "Not yet. He's not . . . he doesn't even know I've been looking for jobs."

"Oh, Zoey, call that man. Tell him what's going on. He'll understand."

He would. Zoey knew he would, though a part of her almost wished he wouldn't just to make leaving a little easier. But no matter how much she loved being with Harry, she couldn't shake the feeling that if she turned her back on Chicago, she'd always regret it.

CHAPTER 14

HARRY PULLED OUT HIS phone as soon as the plane hit the tarmac. He'd had to take an impromptu trip up to Portland to meet a family his show was featuring in a special on-location episode of *Right-On Renovations*. With two special needs kids, the family had been trying to make life work living in a house with too many stairs, and doorways and hallways that were too narrow for the wheelchairs the children used. Harry didn't often agree to filming away from home; this was a detailed project that would require him to be gone for several weeks. But after meeting the family, any doubts he'd harbored had disappeared. They needed help, and he was happy to be involved.

He wasn't sure what he'd do with the kids. Bring them along, probably. His show would help him find someone to watch them while he was filming. A sudden desire to ask Zoey swelled inside him. What if she came with him to Portland? She could keep the kids while he was working, then they'd all be together during his downtime. Like a family.

Zoey had mentioned that Ms. Emily's home healthcare nurse was only staying through the following week. That had to mean she was good to be on her own. Would Zoey be willing to leave her? Filming in Portland didn't start for another couple of weeks. Surely she would at least feel ready by then.

With his phone out of airplane mode, it dinged with the messages and texts he'd missed during the flight.

The kids were fine. His mom had been with them in the hours Zoey hadn't covered the past couple of days.

There had been a minor emergency during demo of *Right-On*'s current project—the young couple remodeling grandma's house—but Jason had handled it while Harry was still in the air and all was under control.

Zoey had texted, asking him to let her know when he landed, and could she come over to see him later?

He quickly responded to Zoey's message. *Just landed. I'll be home by ten. I'd love to see you.* He pushed his phone back into his pocket and stood, retrieving his bag from the overhead bin, a burst of sudden energy in his step. After a long day, time with Zoey was exactly what he needed.

Later, after checking on his sleeping kids and thanking his Mom for basically moving in for the past two days before sending her on her way, he waited anxiously for Zoey to arrive. As soon as her car pulled into the drive, he moved to the front door, opening it when she was only halfway up the walk.

He hurried out to meet her, wrapping her up in an enormous

hug before pressing his lips to hers. "I missed you," he said, his hands still around her waist.

She smiled. "I missed you too."

"Come on." He led her inside. "How are you? How have things been?"

"Your mom is great," Zoey said. "It was fun hanging out with her a little bit."

"Yeah, she loves being with the kids." They moved into the living room and settled onto the couch. "Do you want anything? Something to drink?"

Zoey shook her head. "I'm good. Have you ever thought about asking your mom to keep the kids full time?"

"Thought about it, yes. But she doesn't have the endurance for it, I don't think. Plus, Charlotte needs her too. If she were with my kids all the time, she'd have less time to be with Charlotte's kids." Harry leaned back onto the couch and extended an arm to Zoey. She nestled in, wrapping an arm around his waist and resting her head on his shoulder. "How are *you*, though?" he asked again. "You never answered my question."

She lifted her head, raising a hand to guide his face down to hers. Her kiss felt urgent, almost pleading, and when she took a breath, it caught in her throat, stuttering out like she was close to tears. "Harry, I have to tell you something," she finally said.

Harry tensed, but willed his heart to settle. There was no reason to panic yet. "Okay. You know you can tell me anything."

She sat up, pulling her hands into her lap and took a deep breath. "I have a job interview on Wednesday. In Chicago."

"Okay," Harry said slowly. "I, um, I didn't know you were already looking."

Zoey shrugged. "But, we did know this was temporary."

"We knew you taking care of the kids was temporary. I didn't think *we* were."

"That's not what I'm saying either. I don't want things to end between us. But I feel like I have to do this. A colleague gave me a heads-up weeks ago, right before you and I started seeing each other. I sent over my resume and honestly didn't give it much thought after that." She nudged him with her knee. "I was kind of preoccupied with you, and the kids. But then they asked me to come in for an interview, and . . . I can't say no, Harry."

She *couldn't*? Or she just didn't want to? "Will you take it if they offer you the job?"

She only hesitated a moment. "It's a good job. My dream job, really. Evening news in one of the biggest media markets in the country? It's a once-in-a-lifetime offer. *Nobody* gets these jobs before they're thirty. Nobody."

Harry leaned forward, propping his elbows up on his knees. "What about us?"

Zoey took a long time to respond. "Like I said. I don't want things to change between us."

And yet, she wanted to move a thousand miles away. Things *would* change whether she wanted them to or not.

"Have you thought about looking for a job here in L.A.? I get that this is your decision, but would you even consider it?" He'd posed the question before and she'd dodged around actually providing an answer.

"Do you know how competitive the industry is in L.A.? There is no city as full of beautiful people hoping to be on television, hoping to make it onto a national broadcast. I could get a job here, for sure, but it probably wouldn't be more than doing four a.m. traffic updates or something as equally ridiculous. It would be nothing compared to what this job in Chicago would be."

"But you have to start somewhere, right? And you're good at what you do. It wouldn't take you long."

"But I already did start somewhere. In Chicago. It's my home. People know my name there, and they're willing to give me this chance. I feel like walking away would be turning my back on everything I've worked so hard to build."

It's not that Harry didn't get what she was saying. He understood what it felt like to work to make a name for yourself, to build a career. But Zoey was acting like there wasn't any crossover between markets. That news stations in Los Angeles wouldn't consider the experience she'd gained working in Chicago.

"I should have told you sooner," Zoey said. "I'm sorry to leave you hanging with the kids. I know Charlotte isn't in a position to help out with them right now."

"It doesn't matter," Harry said. "Hannah starts school soon and Oliver will be in preschool. I'll figure something out until then."

"Will you take them to Portland with you?" Zoey asked.

He'd texted her about the reason for his trip and the possibility of doing an on-location shoot. He almost laughed at her question. To think that he'd hoped they might *all* go to Portland together. "I think so, yeah. They might have to miss the first week of school, but I don't want to leave them at home." He looked up and caught her eye. "I was going to ask you if you wanted to go, too. But I guess that isn't likely now, huh?"

Her shoulders fell. "It's not that easy. I would *love* to be in Portland with you and the kids. But—" She pushed her face into her hands. "I don't know how to explain this without sounding like a terrible person."

"How about you just say it?" Harry said, an edge to his voice. "I'm a grownup, Zoey. I can take it."

"I've been living your life, Harry. Working in your house, hanging out with your kids, attending events for your work. And it's been amazing. But it almost feels like I've forgotten who I am. When we went to the zoo last week, everyone knew who you were. I know you said I'd get used to ignoring the fans, and I'm sure I would, but . . . Harry, I didn't matter. I was faceless. Nameless—"

"Not to me," he said, interrupting her. "Is that what this is about? The attention? The fans?"

"No. That's not what I'm saying. It just made me realize how much I miss my job. I miss the intensity and the pace and the opportunity to use *my* voice in a way that matters. I want to be more than just the person that happens to be with you."

Harry sensed there was something Zoey wasn't saying. It was

as if her words on the surface made sense, but there was a layer of emotion underneath that was bigger than the words. No matter how hard she tried to keep her voice controlled—and she was trying, he could tell—he could still hear the emotion spilling over, breaking through the cracks.

"I still don't understand why you couldn't find work here. L .A. stations will consider the experience you gained in Chicago. You wouldn't be starting over. Or what if you started something new? I could easily get you a job on my show. I could even get you a screentest with the network for hosting something. There are always new shows popping up."

Zoey froze and Harry immediately realized he'd said the wrong thing. "I'm a journalist, Harry. I don't *want* to work on your show. That's almost as bad as what the other moms at the park suggested. One of them asked why I even needed to keep working at all. I'm *the* Harrison Beckford's girlfriend. Shouldn't that be enough?"

Harry rolled his eyes. "That's ridiculous. Who cares what those women think? That's not what *I* think."

"But you kind of do. You just dismissed my entire career in two sentences, Harry."

"That's not what I meant to do. I just want to be with you. I'm trying to think of ways to make that possible."

Zoey stood up and crossed to the window that looked out into the backyard. It was too dark for her to see anything, but she stood there anyway, staring for at least a minute before finally turning around. "I don't think you realize how easy it was to fall into your life. You're amazing, you know? Your kids are amazing, and the house is amazing and it's just all so . . ." She breathed out a sigh. "You're everything I could ever imagine wanting for myself. Add on the glamour and the money and the red-carpet events and the attention? It's like a fairy tale, Harry. You're like a fairy tale."

"And yet, you're still leaving."

She crossed the room and sat down beside him, reaching for his hands. "I'm afraid that if I stay, if I don't go play out this part of my life, that one day, when I'm used to all this," she motioned to the room around her, "I might resent you for it. That I'll resent giving up everything in *my* life to live in yours."

Harry pulled his hands away from Zoey's grasp. The conversation felt all too familiar. It wasn't all that long ago that his ex-wife had said something similar. It wasn't the life she would have chosen, and she didn't want to resent him, or the kids, for forcing her to be something she wasn't. He scoffed and shook his head. "You sound just like Samantha."

"Harry. That's not fair. That's not what's happening here. Your kids aren't *my* kids. You aren't my husband. We've only been together a couple of months. It's not the same thing."

Maybe not. But her leaving sure felt the same. "I don't want you to worry about the kids anymore." Harry stood up and crossed the room, his back to Zoey. "Even if you come back after the interview. If you're here at all, I think it's better that you don't see them."

"What, like, ever? Just like that? I understand that you'll need to find someone else to be their nanny. But I can't even see them? I don't leave until Tuesday morning. At least let me come stay with them on Monday."

Harry shook his head. "It's not a good idea. The more time you spend with them, the more it will hurt when you *aren't* here anymore."

"Okay. So forget about the job. What about us? Will you even try to make a long-distance relationship work?"

Harry shook his head. "It isn't just about me. Don't you get that? You're asking to have a long-distance relationship with the entire family. I can't do that to them. They already have a mom that lives on the other side of the country. Plus, my schedule is so carefully balanced, Zoey. I've fought for every evening, every weekend that I can for my kids. I can't throw in flights to Chicago whenever I want to see you."

"You don't even want to wait and see what happens? I might not get the job. This is my one chance. If it doesn't work out, there likely won't be another opportunity like this for a long time. I could come back free and clear. We could still be together."

Harry turned to face her. "I don't want to be a consolation prize, Zoey. And I know how competitive you are. If you don't get this job, you won't stop looking for another one. I can't risk the kids' hearts on a *might*."

"So that's it? We're over?"

"You tell me!" He put his hands on his hips. "I already know what I want. I want you. I realize I'm asking you to move your life across the country. It sucks that it has to be that way, but it is what it is. I have the kids. I have my show. I can't move." He sighed and shook his head. "I guess a part of me hoped I'd be worth the effort. Worth moving for. I hoped I'd be enough. But if it isn't clear to you, I'm not going to pressure you into it. I already *know* what it feels like to have someone resent you for giving them a life they didn't want." He held his hands up and backed away, moving toward the kitchen. "I won't do it again."

Tears pooled in Zoey's eyes and flowed down her cheeks, making Harry's heart lurch. A part of him ached to hold her, to run to her and wrap her up in his arms. But he couldn't do it. She'd tapped too close to the pain and rejection he'd felt during his divorce. "You know the way out," he said softly before turning and heading to his room.

CHAPTER 15

ZOEY PULLED HER KEYS out of her purse and moved toward the door, but then she paused. She stared at the keys in her hand. They weren't really her keys, were they? Even the car she'd been driving the past couple of months belonged to him.

Zoey dropped the keys onto the entryway table and slipped out the door.

It took half an hour to walk back to Nana's house. She'd thought about calling an Uber a time or two, but the walking seemed to help her process what had just happened, so she'd pushed on.

Breaking up was not what she had expected when she'd driven to Harry's. She'd expected him to understand. To support her need to live her *own* life, to pursue *her* dreams. Was it his celebrity that made him so selfish? That made him expect her to just fall in with his carefully crafted existence? He'd made himself clear though. She wasn't worth a flight to Chicago. She worked herself into his life, or they couldn't be together.

So fine.

They wouldn't be.

Pain gripped at Zoey's heart as the realization pounded through her brain.

They wouldn't be together. But that didn't mean she cared about him any less.

As Zoey approached Nana's front door, she wiped away her lingering tears and willed her emotions into order. Her mother was right inside; she was the last person Zoey wanted to talk to about Harrison. Sadly, Zoey didn't much want to talk to Nana about him either. She wouldn't understand at all and would absolutely try and convince Zoey to give up on Chicago and make a career for herself in L.A.. Nana was very persuasive. A conversation with her wasn't a risk Zoey could take.

As much as her heart hurt, as much as she longed for a way to make her relationship with Harry work, she'd never forgive herself if she didn't at least try for the Channel 4 job. She'd worked too hard, put in too many hours to walk away.

Both women were still up when Zoey let herself into the house, despite the late hour. Nana looked like she was dozing in her chair; Zoey's mom sat on the couch beside her, her legs curled up under her and her iPad in her lap. Zoey dropped into the chair across from her, grateful for the dim lighting. If she stayed in the shadows her mother might not notice she'd been crying. Still, could she avoid conversation for three more days? Her flight wasn't supposed to leave until Tuesday morning, but truly, what would she do if she stayed in California? Just sit around and miss Harry, probably.

"Hi," her mother said, her voice low. "You okay?"

Zoey nodded. "Yeah. Just tired."

"How's the boyfriend?" her mother said, her voice all sing-songy and happy.

"Fine, I guess."

"I bet he's going to miss you when you're back in Chicago. I was just thinking it's a good thing he's got the money to handle all the traveling back and forth. And he'll obviously pay for your flights too—"

"Mom." Zoey kept her voice calm. This wasn't a conversation she wanted to have with her mother, but it was better than letting her go on and on about a relationship that didn't exist anymore.

"What?" her mother said, her tone impatient.

"We broke up. He doesn't want a long-distance relationship. He said it would be too hard on the kids."

Her mother's face fell. "Then why are you leaving?"

Zoey stood up and moved toward her bedroom. "I'm not going to try and explain it to you, Mom. I know you won't get it."

"Try me," her mother said, following behind her. "Don't assume, Zoey. That's not fair to me."

"I *want* this job, Mom," Zoey said, spinning around to face her. "What else do you want me to say? I love Harry, but this is what I've been working for. I can't give it up. Even for a man as wonderful as he is."

Her mother frowned. "A man like him might not come along again."

A man like him would never come along again. And a not-so-tiny part of Zoey worried that she was walking away from something better than anything she'd ever find again. But she bristled at the idea that it had to be all or nothing. And that idea was enough to compel her competitive heart right back to Chicago where she'd earn her way on her own merits, and not just because someone who'd already made his way decided to include her in his life.

"I know, Mom. I know." Zoey looked back over her mother's shoulder into the living room. "Can you help Nana get to bed tonight? I'm going to go to bed."

Her mother followed her gaze, nodding. "Of course," she said, though she still followed Zoey into her bedroom. She stood in the doorway, her iPad clutched to her chest.

Zoey pulled her phone out of her purse, plugging it in on the nightstand before dropping onto the bed.

"I've been watching old news clips," her mother said. She swallowed, her eyes trained on the floor. "Clips of you."

Zoey stilled. "Why?"

Her mom took a deep breath. "I know you think I don't care, Zoey. Mom told me you said—" She sniffed and ran her hand across her cheeks.

Was she crying? A pang of emotion pricked Zoey's chest.

"I'm proud of you," her mom continued. "So proud. I told

my friends all the time they had to watch Channel 11 because you would give them the news straight. Of course I want you to get married. I'm not going to lie about that. You're pushing thirty, Zoey. It's time to get serious about this."

Zoey held up her hands; she really wasn't up for the pushing thirty narrative.

"Just let me finish," Mom said. "Having said that—and I only say it because I love you—I'm sorry if I ever made you feel like your career wasn't important. I just want you to be happy. Whatever makes you that way, that's what I want."

"But you still think I should stay in California to be with Harry."

Her mother stretched her lips into a tight line. "I want you to do whatever is going to make you happy."

Zoey would give her mom props for trying, but what she really thought was written all over her face. Too tired to argue, Zoey hugged her mom, promised her that she wasn't mad and that she'd stop avoiding her phone calls, then settled onto her bed, wishing she could turn off her brain.

She kept reliving her conversation with Harry over and over again. That he had so quickly suggested that she walk away from her career and just work with him on his show stung worst of all. Did no one value what she'd built for herself? Did no one want her to maximize her own potential?

Zoey turned on her laptop and pulled up the flight information for her trip back to Chicago, suddenly feeling like she couldn't get out of L.A. fast enough. She clicked through a few options then stared at the screen, weighing her decision.

Eighty bucks to change her flight from the following Tuesday to tomorrow morning?

Totally worth it.

Zoey had sublet her apartment when she'd left Chicago. One of her former coworkers at the station was married to a real estate agent who managed short term rentals and had quickly found someone to lease the space for a couple of months. Fortuitously, when she landed back in Chicago, her space had just been vacated. It had only taken a quick text to ask the realtor to leave it empty for her. She'd never been so happy to enter her own apartment. She'd expected it to still have tenants, which would have left her living in a hotel.

Before leaving the city at the end of the summer, she'd turned the guest bedroom of her apartment into an "owner's closet," locking all of her work clothes and personal belongings that she didn't take with her to California into the space. A wardrobe rack next to the window held most of her work clothes. She riffled through them, wondering which would work best for her interview.

Her hand stopped on a red, cropped jacket she'd often paired with her favorite black pencil skirt. She pulled it out, then slammed it back onto the rack with an eye roll. Would she ever escape her mother's opinions? She reached for a high-necked, sleeveless royal blue dress with wide, white bands trimming either side of the dress, from armpit to hem like racing stripes. The dress made her feel like a million bucks. She told herself she would have picked it even without her mother's unsolicited commentary, but Zoey wasn't so sure. As gentle as her mother's voice was, it was still just. *so. loud.*

Zoey carried the dress back to her bedroom, hanging it in her mostly empty closet. She had a lot more space in her Chicago apartment than she'd had in Nana's tiny front bedroom, but she missed the efficiency of the shelves Harry had installed.

She also missed Harry. Even though it hadn't even been twenty-four hours since she'd seen him last, the emotional distance between them made everything that much more painful. She pulled her phone out of her purse and stared at the screen. Should she text him? Let him know she'd left earlier than she'd planned?

She couldn't think of a reason why he'd care. He'd already told her he didn't need her help with the kids anymore.

Still. She'd left the state. She owed him a text at least, didn't she?

Hi. Just wanted you to know I'm already in Chicago. I miss you. I love you. Please don't give up on me.

No, no, no, no, no. Zoey deleted the message and tried again.

Just wanted you to know I'm in Chicago already. Good luck with your filming in Portland.

Too impersonal? Why did it have to be so hard? She deleted one more time.

I'm sorry things ended the way they did. I'm in Chicago. I already miss you.

Too much? Maybe, but Zoey couldn't think about it anymore, so she sent the text and tossed her phone onto the bed behind her.

Three minutes later, three hours later, even three days later when Zoey was finished with her interview and out to drinks with the Channel 4 producers who had all but explicitly promised her the evening anchor position, all she could think about was the fact that Harry had never texted back.

She ran into Veronica Darling on her way out of the restaurant.

"Zoey!" Veronica said, rushing up to her. She air-kissed either side of Zoey's face then leaned back, a huge smile across her face. "I heard you were in town. You're going for the Channel 4 anchor job, right?"

Zoey eyed her curiously. Veronica seemed surprisingly nonchalant about the possibility of Zoey getting the job. "Yes. But, aren't you, also?"

Veronica shook her head. "Not anymore. Phil got a job offer that's too amazing to pass up. We're moving in a couple of weeks."

"Oh," Zoey said, feeling suddenly uncomfortable. She had no idea who Phil actually was. "Um, Phil?"

"What? Oh. I guess it's been a while since we've talked. Phil is my fiancé." She held out her hand, flashing a rock the size of New Jersey.

"Wow. Congratulations."

"We met at a coffee shop," Veronica said. "It was totally cheesy and romantic and blah, blah, blah, here we are six months later."

"I mean, that's amazing. And now you're moving?"

"Crazy, right? We'll be back next summer for the wedding. But we're going to Miami, of all places. Can you believe it? I'm so excited to be somewhere warm. And I've already reached out to a few stations and have some interviews lined up. I mean, I won't get an anchor position, not right away, but honestly, I'll cover Friday night high school football if it means I can spend my mornings lounging on the beach. And the job is so great for Phil. We're really excited."

"That's great," Zoey said. "Truly. A shame about the anchor job here, though."

Veronica shrugged dismissively. "I'm not worried about it. Now that you're back in town, they're going to give it to you anyway."

"I'm happy for you," Zoey said. "I hope you love Miami. I guess I'll think about you in December when it's five degrees here."

Veronica laughed. "Or just come see me. I will not miss Chicago winters, that's for sure."

Zoey said goodbye and caught a cab home. She usually pulled out her phone the second her butt landed in a cab just to keep herself occupied enough that the driver never felt like starting a conversation. But tonight she left her phone in her bag. She stared out the window, watching as the city flew past her window.

Veronica made it seem so easy. Even though she'd been working, building her career for years, it didn't even seem like she'd hesitated to give it all up for her fiancé's work. Well, and for seventy-degree Decembers.

"You okay?" her cab driver asked, glancing at her through the rearview mirror.

"Hmm?" Zoey asked.

"You look . . . pensive. Contemplative," he said. "Just asking if you're okay."

"Oh. Yes. Thank you."

"You're that lady on the news, right? Channel 12?"

Heat warmed Zoey's cheeks. It had been a while since anyone had recognized her. "Yes. I mean, not anymore. I'm still on the news. Just a different station."

"Big job, handling the news like you do. You ever meet anyone famous?"

Zoey smiled. "Sometimes. I interviewed Michael Jordan once."

"No kidding? Nice guy?"

She nodded. "Very. What about you? You ever pick up anyone famous?"

"A few times. You know the guy that wrote Hamilton? He rode in my cab. And I drove President Obama once, back before he was President."

"Really? How did you remember him? I mean, if he wasn't president yet, he was just some guy, right?"

"I never forget a face," the driver said. "It's just the way I am. Plus, he had a lot to say, Obama did. He told me he was going to run for president one day. Then what do you know? He did it."

Zoey smiled. "I like that story."

They pulled to a stop at a red light next to a city bus.

The driver pointed at the ad painted on the side of the bus. "Hey. There's another one. That guy was in my cab yesterday. He's maybe not as famous as Obama, but he's still got his face on the side of a bus so that's something, yeah? He's on TV like you. One of those home-renovation shows."

Zoey slowly turned, taking in the perfectly chiseled, slightly scruffy, intensely gorgeous face of Harrison Beckford filling the oversized advertising space on the side of the bus. Her heart pounded in her chest. First of all, how had she not noticed that Harrison's face was on the side of all the buses in Chicago? Second, Harrison himself was *in* the city? Zoey had so many questions.

"Harrison Beckford?" she said to the driver, her words measured and slow. Maybe the driver would say no. Maybe he would laugh dismissively and say, "Just kidding! Wouldn't that have been funny though?" Maybe he would say he'd been mistaken, and it hadn't been him after all.

"Yeah," the driver said. "That's him."

"He was in your cab? Here in Chicago?"

The driver tossed her a funny look. "Where else?"

Zoey couldn't think. She could scarcely breath. Why was Harry in Chicago? First her conversation with Veronica and now this? It felt like the universe was trying to give her a massive, in-your-face wake-up call. What were the odds that she would get in the same cab that had driven Harry not even twenty-four hours ago? What were the freaking odds?

But then, if he'd been in the city at least twenty-four hours, why hadn't he called her? Was he there for another reason? He'd never mentioned traveling to Chicago for work before. He *had* to be there to see her.

"Did he happen to mention why he was in the city?" Zoey asked, leaning forward.

"Who?"

"Harrison Beckford," Zoey answered, hoping her impatience didn't sound in her voice.

"Oh. No. Didn't say much of anything. Gave me a huge tip, though."

Zoey finally pulled out her phone, staring at the screen as if that alone was enough to make Harry reach out to her.

Because she couldn't reach out to him.

He had no idea she even knew he was in town. If he wanted to see her, he'd call. Wouldn't he?

The cab stopped in front of Zoey's building. She dug through her purse for her wallet, realizing as she pulled out the cash that her hands were trembling. She handed over the money then climbed out of the car but didn't immediately go into her building.

Did Harrison know where she lived? He could have gotten the address from Nana or her mother. Oh, her mother would have loved the drama of that. Harrison coming over, begging for her address so he could chase her down. Was he planning to surprise her?

Zoey looked up and down the street, half-expecting to see him hiding behind a trash can or sitting casually at one of the café tables that lined the street. But nothing looked out of the ordinary.

The crosswalk to Zoey's left blinked and changed and a rush of pedestrians moved across the street. Zoey backed up, pressing her back against the front of her building and looked at her phone. She called Nana first. She'd likely have an easier time discerning the truth from her, than from Mom.

"Hey Zoey," Nana said. "How's my girl?" It hadn't even been a week and Zoey already missed talking to Nana every day. "Hey, Nana. If I ask you a question, do you promise to answer me honestly?"

"Sure, baby. What else would I do?"

"Did Harrison tell you he was coming to Chicago?"

Nana paused, but the surprise in her voice sounded genuine when she finally spoke. "What?"

"I think he's here. In the city. Do you know anything about him coming? Did he ask you for my address? Anything?"

"No, sweetie. I haven't seen Harry in over a week. Since before you left. Want me to ask your mother?"

"No. If you haven't seen him, I'm sure she hasn't either."

"Why do you think he's in the city?"

"It's nothing," Zoey said quickly, suddenly feeling foolish. "I thought I—I'm sure it was just a mistake." It occurred to Zoey how likely it *was* a mistake. It could have just been someone that looked like Harry.

"Want me to call him and ask him?"

"No!" Zoey said quickly. If *she* didn't have the guts to call him, she for sure didn't want her grandma to do it for her. "Sorry. I didn't mean to yell. But no. I'll handle it."

"Have you heard from him at all?"

Zoey took a deep breath. "No. But he was pretty final about how he left things. I really didn't expect to." She had, though. When she'd texted him that first day in the city, she'd fully expected him to text her back.

"I wish you wouldn't give up, Zoey. I think you two are really meant for each other."

"I know, Nana. I know."

Later that night, Zoey finally got up the courage to reach out to Harry.

Are you in Chicago? she texted. She sat the phone down on her coffee table face up and stared at the screen, willing him to respond. But still, nothing came through. One minute turned into two, and then three as she sat, unmoving, and stared at her phone, tapping the screen every minute or so to refresh the screen and keep it on. Once, after five minutes of waiting, the little floating dots that indicated someone was typing a message danced at the bottom of her screen.

Her heart climbed into her throat and she nearly screamed, but then the dots disappeared, and no message ever arrived.

Dejected, Zoey tossed her phone onto the couch and

stomped into her bathroom, angrily yanking on the handle to turn on her shower. The nozzle broke off in her hand, but not before the water turned on, dumping an endless—and unstoppable—stream of ice-cold water into the tub.

Zoey dropped onto the side of the tub, the hot tears streaming down her face a contrast to the plink, plink of cold water splashing from the tub onto her arm and shoulder. At least the emergent situation kept her from feeling sorry for herself for too long. The water was draining, but not quite as fast as the tub was filling. If she didn't get help quick, she'd have a much bigger problem on her hands.

Sighing, she kicked off her heels and ran for her phone, dialing the super's number even as she raced across the hall to her neighbor's apartment, still holding the faucet handle she'd broken off.

Her neighbor, Ryan, opened the door, wearing pajama pants and a t-shirt and looking very much like she'd gotten him out of bed. She glanced at her watch. It wasn't that late, just past ten, but her neighbors were both schoolteachers. An early bedtime made sense for them.

Zoey held up the faucet, the sound of running water audible through her open apartment door. "Help?" she said hopefully.

Ryan looked from Zoey, to the faucet handle, then back to Zoey, his eyes blinking several times. "Ryan?" Zoey said. "You okay?"

"Sorry. Just trying to wake up. I don't know how to fix that. But Daren will. Let me get him."

"Thank you!" Zoey called to his retreating form.

"Did you call the super?" Daren said, as Zoey followed him back to her apartment.

She nodded. "Yeah. He didn't answer."

The bathtub was already half-full when they made it into the bathroom, but it only took Daren a second to turn the water off. He held up the pliers he'd used to manually twist the valve closed. "Glad I brought these with me."

"How did you *know* to bring them with you?" Zoey asked.

"It happened at our place not that long ago. It's the same faucet. I made a lucky guess."

Zoey heaved a sigh. She shouldn't be so tired. She'd gotten plenty of sleep the past few nights. But her emotional exhaustion felt bone deep. "Thanks, Daren. Sorry to pull you out of bed."

"No worries," he said. "I'll fall back to sleep quick." They walked together to her apartment door. "Ryan, on the other hand, might be up until tomorrow. He's terrible at going back to sleep."

"Oh, no. I'm so sorry," Zoey said. "I panicked. I didn't know what else to do."

Daren reached out and squeezed her shoulder. "Don't worry about it. He'll be fine." He leaned against the door jamb. "Hey, are you back for good?"

Zoey's eyes dropped to the floor. "I don't know. I think so. I'm going to do a few guest spots as evening news anchor for Channel 4. If it goes well, they're saying the job is mine."

"Hey, well done," Daren said. "That's amazing."

"Yeah, thanks," Zoey said, though she hardly sounded enthusiastic.

"I guess I was curious if the thing with the guy from TV meant you'd be staying in L.A. permanently."

A thread of discomfort wound through her belly. She hadn't actually had a conversation with her neighbors, which meant they'd had to have gotten their information off the internet.

"Sorry," Daren said, clearly sensing her discomfort. "Is that weird that I said something? Ryan and I kind of had a freak out moment when we saw your picture come up on *Entertainment Tonight*."

"It's fine," Zoey said. "Still just a little weird to know that people know about that even without me telling anyone."

"I'm sure," Daren said. "You looked gorgeous though. Like you belonged together. I hope it works out for you guys."

"Yeah. I don't . . . I don't think it's going to. I don't know. Maybe. It's complicated."

"Isn't it always?" Daren said. "I didn't expect him to be quite so tall in person, but girl, that is one seriously fine man. I'd say well done if the look in your eyes wasn't saying that complicated actually means painful."

It took Zoey a second to process what Daren had said. "Wait. Did you just say *in person*? Have you *seen* him somewhere?"

Daren looked at her like she'd asked him to sing his ABCs while doing the chicken dance. "He was outside your apartment this afternoon. I assumed he was on his way in or out."

"Oh, geez." Zoey leaned against the wall. "He was here? *Here, here*? Did he say anything?"

"You didn't *know* he was here?"

She only managed to shake her head.

"That explains why he looked so nervous."

She pressed a hand to her forehead. "I haven't heard from him in days. He hasn't called, or texted. I can't believe he's actually *here*."

Daren shrugged. "Maybe he wants to surprise you?"

"I wish he'd get on with it, then. The cab driver that brought me home tonight told me Harry rode in his cab yesterday. *Here.* In Chicago. I thought the guy was mistaken. It was just someone that looked like him. But I guess not."

"You call him Harry?" Daren said, his voice all sappy and sentimental. "That's so sweet."

She shot him a look and he schooled his features. "Sorry. Not the time. That's crazy that you rode in the same cab."

"It's like the universe is playing some cruel game of hide and seek. Even though I *left*, I can't seem to get away from him. And seriously. What are the odds? The same cab? Chicago has millions of cabs."

"Maybe not millions. And drivers often stay in the same parts of the city. He was somewhere around your apartment building, it's maybe not *that* crazy. But still. I see your point."

That maybe made a little bit of sense. Zoey had ridden in cabs with the same driver before on her way to or from work. But it was still pretty unbelievable.

"Do you mind if I ask why you *did* leave?" Daren asked. "You weren't leaving *him*, were you?"

Zoey didn't answer. How could she?

"It's complicated?" Daren finally asked.

"Yeah," Zoey said with a sigh.

"Hang in there," Daren said, giving her arm one more squeeze. "And text the super about your faucet. It's not a hard fix, but you shouldn't use your shower until he takes care of it."

Zoey nodded. At least she had a guest bathroom she could use. "Thanks. Please tell Ryan I'm sorry I woke him up. I owe you guys."

After texting the super, Zoey pulled up her text thread with Harry and stared at his *lack* of response. So he *was* in Chicago. Somewhere close enough that he'd been at her apartment a few hours before.

Why hadn't he responded? If he'd come all this way, if he'd made the effort to find her apartment, why not respond to her text? She sent one more message, promising herself that if he didn't respond after this one, she'd be done.

My neighbors told me they saw you today. Are you still in town? Can I see you?

She plugged the phone in next to her bed and gathered her things to haul them to the tiny guest bathroom on the other side of the apartment. Even after her shower, Harry still hadn't responded.

Zoey curled up under her comforter and turned off her lamp, willing herself to forget Harry long enough to get some sleep.

Try as she might to turn her brain off, one thought kept pushing to the surface. This was not what going home to Chicago was supposed to feel like.

CHAPTER 16

HARRY SAT IN Ms. Emily's kitchen, his head between his hands. "I just couldn't do it," he said. It had been three weeks since he'd flown to Chicago and then home again. He hadn't been to see Ms. Emily in all that time. It was a cowardly thing to do, but he was almost embarrassed to face her. He'd stood outside Zoey's apartment door. He'd sat in the lobby of her building. He'd ridden in cabs around and around her block. But he'd never gotten up the courage to see her. As time went by, he felt more and more foolish, so much that it not only kept him from texting Zoey again, but from seeing Ms. Emily as well.

"I guess when I saw her apartment, her neighbors, when I envisioned her life in Chicago, I realized she was right. I *was* expecting her to leave her life behind. I wasn't thinking about what was really on the line. I acted like the only thing she had going on that didn't revolve around me was taking care of you." Harry looked up. "Not that you weren't the most important thing."

Ms. Emily smiled. "I know what you mean."

"I think I screwed up," Harry said. "I should have supported her doing the interview. I should have told her I was willing to make it work, even if she did have to move back to Chicago. I mean, I wouldn't want to do long distance forever, but I shouldn't have pressured her to make a final decision so soon. I should have been willing to give her space, to support her career choices."

"You have to understand, Harry. Zoey feels a lot of pressure from her mother to get married, to have a family. And she wants those things, too. But she's always fought hard against the idea that that's *all* she was meant to do. She's always been a dreamer. She wanted to make something of herself. To make a difference in the world. Then she lost her job and I think it shook her. When she moved out here, she found a new version of herself in the life she shared with you. I think it scared her how much she loved it. Maybe it felt like she had to choose."

"But it doesn't have to be one or the other, does it?" Harry asked. "I would never expect her to walk away from something that's important to her."

Ms. Emily cocked her head. "Wouldn't you?"

Harry's gut tightened. He *had* asked her to give it all up. Had dismissed what was important to her in a matter of words. "It isn't what I meant to do. I would never expect her to give up her career."

"I'm sure that's true. I think Zoey will figure out that she doesn't have to pick one or the other. She might just need a little time."

Harry shook his head. "I don't know. She told me it was her dream job. And now she's got it. I've been watching clips, as many as I can get my hands on, and she's really good at what she does. Plus, she seems happy."

"Harry. A news broadcast is not an accurate reflection of her emotions."

Ms. Emily made a good point. But Zoey *did* look happy. There was a light in her eyes, cheesy as that sounded. She seemed content. Harry thought of the three-word response he'd sent her the last time she'd texted him, telling him she knew he'd been in Chicago. By the time he'd gotten the message, he'd already landed in L.A..

I'm sorry, Zoey, he had texted.

It was the last time they had communicated.

It hadn't been hard to keep himself busy. He'd taken Hannah and Oliver to Portland for two weeks—his mom had taken some vacation time to come with him—to do the renovation for the special needs family, and then the week after they'd gotten back, Hannah had started kindergarten. Hannah had asked about Zoey enough times that he couldn't forget her completely, but he'd been able to focus on the next thing enough to keep himself from wallowing too completely. Or worse, from reaching out to her and begging her to come back.

Which is exactly what he wanted to do. He never would, though. He'd never risk making her feel like he expected it.

"Have *you* talked to her lately?" he asked, looking up to meet Ms. Emily's eye.

She nodded. "She calls once or twice a week."

"*Is* she happy?"

"Sure. In a way. But I think she misses you too. She's asked about you."

Harry perked up. "What did you tell her?"

"Harrison Beckford. This is not an elementary school playground. I'm not going to play *she said, he said* with you. If you want to talk to Zoey, *call her.*"

Ms. Emily was right, but it was easier said than done. Each day that passed without talking to her made it feel that much harder to initiate a conversation. What would she think? Would she forgive him for showing up in Chicago only to freak out and fly home without seeing her? Would she forgive his insensitivity for suggesting her career wasn't important? Would she still want to see him? Would she want to give him another chance?

If anything was clear, it was that he hated his life without her in it. Things were fine. The show was fine. The kids were fine. His family was fine. But without Zoey in his life, the world had lost its shine.

CHAPTER 17

ZOEY SAT AT THE anchor desk, minutes before going live, and reviewed her notes for the broadcast. It was all pretty straight forward. It had been a relatively slow news day and the headlines were pretty low key, but she was fine with that. They'd been covering a high stakes murder trial the last few weeks; she was ready for something a little tamer. After headlines, they'd be doing an extended weather segment—snow in October was odd, even for Chicago—and then they were airing a pre-taped interview with a Chicago-native author who had written a self-help book. Something about finding your best life through intentional dreams and aspirations.

Zoey wasn't necessarily big on self-help books. At least, she never had been before, but she'd been in the studio when they'd filmed the interview earlier that day and she'd been captivated by something the author had said.

"A poorly defined dream is like a young girl dreaming of

the wedding, without giving any thought to the groom," she had said. "What's a wedding? It's an event. But life isn't about events. It's about people. About connections. What kind of marriage do you want? What kind of job do you want? Dream about what you want to get *out* of your life and let that set your priorities."

Zoey had pulled out her phone and immediately written out what the author had said. There was truth to the words. It resonated in Zoey's gut and spoke to her in a meaningful way. What she couldn't figure out is if that's what *she* had done. Had she dreamed of a job, of accomplishing a thing that no one her age had ever done before just because she liked the thrill of accomplishing something big? Had she thought about what she wanted to actually get out of her life, or had it all just been about the accomplishment?

"Live in sixty seconds," a producer called out, pulling Zoey's attention back to the present.

It had been almost two months since she'd started at Channel 4, and she loved what she did. There was no denying that.

But at the end of the day, at the end of *every* day, Zoey was lonely. And the longer she was away from Harry, the more Zoey was convinced there was only one man that could make that loneliness go away.

"In five, four, three . . ."

Zoey watched her producer count down the last two numbers silently then looked directly into the camera. "Live in Chicago, I'm Zoey Williamson and this is Channel 4 News."

After the broadcast, Zoey snagged a copy of the author's book from the studio. There were several copies laying around—they'd been sent over from the publisher—so she didn't think anyone would miss just one. She took it home, ate leftover Chinese from her fridge while running herself a bath, then settled into the tub and started to read.

"In a world where we are programmed to achieve, achieve, achieve, are we brave enough to acknowledge that what we achieve might not be the thing that makes us happy?" Zoey read out loud. She reached up with her toe and turned on the hot water, running some fresh warmth into her nearly tepid tub. She was shriveled to true raisin status, but she couldn't put the book down long enough to actually get herself out of the water.

She read the line again.

Zoey had been chasing her dream of anchoring the evening news since her first semester of college. And she'd managed to get it. But now what? She'd told Harry she felt like she needed to interview for the job so that she didn't resent him for the lost opportunity. But now she had the opportunity and it didn't feel as good as she had expected it to.

She flipped back a few chapters in the book and found a checklist designed to distill the truth out of any situation. For her, she'd apply the listed questions to her work.

Is it satisfying? Yes.

Do you enjoy it? Yes.

Does it fill you up and make you feel like you matter? Yes and yes.

So far, so good.

The next question read, *Does it bring you joy?*

Zoey dropped the book outside the tub and sank into the water. She was happy when she was at work. But she wasn't sure if, overall, she would say her life had any true joy in it. There was a difference between happiness and joy. Happiness was a tall vanilla cream at Starbucks. But that hardly compared to the feel of Harry's lips on hers, or the sound of Oliver's laughter when she'd tickle him behind his knees.

Was the satisfaction of achieving something wonderful worth leaving behind a continual source of joy in her life? Particularly when, with just a little bit of effort, she could have both?

Because she *could* have both. She'd been so fixated on the possibility of getting the anchor job at Channel 4, she'd dismissed the possibility of working in L.A.

Much of what she'd told Harry about the L.A. industry was true. It would be more competitive. But that didn't mean it would be impossible.

She could try.

But it was almost November.

It had been months since she'd last talked to Harry. Would he even still want her to try? Nothing sounded more terrible than upending her life and moving to California permanently only to have him reject her because he'd fallen in love with someone else. She'd spent weeks agonizing over why he hadn't wanted to actually see her when he came to Chicago. All signs pointed to the possibility that he'd changed his mind about *her.*

Nervous energy coursed through her as she thought about the possibilities. She could text him. Call him. Get on a plane and go and see him.

No. She couldn't go see him. That felt too risky. Nothing said drama like showing up at your old boyfriend's house and having the new girlfriend open the door. It's possible Zoey had watched too many romantic comedies, but that felt like too real of a possibility for her to take that risk.

Calling felt risky as well. What if she said something stupid?

Even though she'd built her career around her ability to speak and communicate clearly, she had zero confidence that in this situation she'd be able to keep it together. And again. Too many movies had awkward phone call scenes.

That left texting. Was it too high school? Maybe. But it also felt . . . safe.

Zoey stood up and reached for a towel, wrapping it around herself as she stepped out of the tub. She grabbed another for her hair, then quickly went through the motions of getting ready for bed, all the while thinking about what she might say if she sent a text.

She thought while she brushed her teeth.

While she flossed and exfoliated and applied lotion to her arms.

She thought while she picked out her pajamas and double checked that her front door was locked and checked again that her balcony door was locked, even though she'd checked it that morning and she was positive she hadn't gone out on the balcony all day.

Finally, when she climbed into bed, she allowed herself to pick up her phone. Chasing a sudden impulse, she texted her mom instead of Harry.

Honest question, she texted. *Do you ever wish you had a different life?*

I need context, her mom immediately responded. *What do you mean?*

Zoey tapped her phone against her lip. *Were me and Nathan enough? Raising us. Was it enough?*

It took her mom a few minutes to respond. Finally a long message came through.

You were more than enough. In hindsight I wish I'd done more to figure out what I liked to do as a person. I was great at being a mom, but I was afraid to be more than that. I got started a little late figuring out who I am as a person, and not just as a mom. I've floundered a little bit the past few years, though the grandkids have helped with that. But I still don't have any regrets, Zoey. You and your brother made me so happy. You're the greatest thing I ever did.

Zoey read the text over and over. It was maybe the most transparent her mother had ever been. *Thanks, Mom,* she replied.

Then she started a new text thread and sent Harry a single word before she could chicken out.

Hi.

CHaPTer 18

Hi.

Harry stared at his phone.

One word.

She'd texted one single word.

For three days he carried that word around in his mind.

What did it mean? How should he respond?

Finally, after three days of agonizing over how—and if—to respond, he texted back.

Hi.

Her response was almost immediate.

That three days of waiting nearly killed me.

He smiled. Another message popped up before he could respond. *I'm nervous,* she had typed.

Well. He could relate to that. *Me too,* he responded.

How are you?

How was he? Could he even answer honestly? He was managing well enough. He had a new nanny who was great, and his sister had gotten far enough along in her pregnancy that she wasn't quite so sick. He'd wrapped up his seventh season of Right-On Renovations, which allowed him more time to work on his product line. The kids were happy enough, though Hannah had a taken a little longer than he'd hoped to get used to kindergarten. Still, she was fine now, so could he even complain? The truth was, whether or not everything else in his life was running smoothly or not hardly mattered at the end of the day. He was off kilter without Zoey. Once he'd gotten used to her daily presence, he couldn't shake how wrong it felt without her around.

He'd thought he was falling in love with her before she left. But her leaving had only confirmed the fact times ten. He loved her. Now more than ever.

It likely didn't help that he ended everyday with her news broadcast. Seeing her face, and hearing her talk kept the memories he had of her real and vivid.

But he couldn't exactly say all that in a text.

I'm surviving, he finally said. It felt true enough.

Just surviving?

Harry dropped onto the couch, pushing aside the blanket and picture books Oliver had left there that morning. *I got a new nanny,* he texted back. *She cooks.*

He leaned back onto the cushions, his heart racing and waited for her to reply.

CHaPTer 19

SHE COOKS?

How was Zoey supposed to respond to that? Congrats on the upgrade? All sorts of uncharitable thoughts pushed through Zoey's mind. She hoped the nanny was ugly. And old. And already married. Oddly, nearly as potent as the sting of Harry potentially caring about someone else—not to imply that Harry had a habit of dating his nannies, but her mind wasn't exactly thinking rationally at the moment—was the sting of the *kids* caring about someone else. She missed them. *Really* missed them.

Before Zoey could respond, Harry sent another message. *I've been watching your broadcasts.*

Zoey couldn't stop herself from smiling. That was a subject change she could appreciate.

You're really good, Zoe, his next message read.

Zoey looked at the time on her phone. She had to be at the

station in an hour. But maybe that still left her enough time. She raced to her front door and flung it open, crossing quickly to Daren and Ryan's apartment. She knocked on the door, realizing too late they might not be home from school yet.

The elevator dinged behind her, and Zoey turned around. When the doors slid open, she sighed with relief. "Oh, I'm so glad you guys are home. I need your help."

It made Zoey sad to think she'd taken so long to get to know her neighbors a little bit. She'd always been on friendly speaking terms with Ryan and Daren, even on come-help-me-fix-my-faucet terms. But they'd only recently started really talking. Spending time together. The two of them had become the only two people, outside of Nana, that knew the full story of what had happened with Harry.

Ryan's eyebrows went up. "What happened?"

"I texted him," Zoey said. "And he texted back and now I have no idea what I should say."

"You should say you love him, and you'll be on the next flight," Daren said.

Zoey followed them into their apartment and leaned against the counter, watching as they unloaded a bag of groceries. "I can't just come right out and say it. Tell me how to do this smoothly. I don't want to mess this up."

Ryan held out his hand for her phone. "What have you said so far?"

Zoey handed him the phone, chewing on her lip until he'd read through the last few messages. "Oh, he's watching Chicago news so he can see you. That's so sweet."

"What do I say?" Zoey reached for her phone. "It's been too long. If I don't respond soon he might get busy doing something else."

"Say thank you, first of all," Daren said. "He paid you a really nice compliment. Then tell him you love him, and you'll be on the next flight."

"Daren!" Zoey said. "That isn't helpful."

He rolled his eyes. "Ask about the kids. If you want to ease in, that's probably a pretty safe topic."

"Right," Zoey said. "The kids. I can definitely ask about the kids."

Thank you, she texted. *How are the kids?*

They miss you, Harry's message read. *Almost as much as I do.*

Zoey gasped. She handed the phone to Ryan and Daren. They read the message and then emitted simultaneous and identical, "Awwww"s.

Ryan handed her phone back. "Zoey," he said calmly. "Don't text him back. *Call him.*"

CHaPTer 20

HARRY'S PHONE LIT UP with an incoming call and his lungs jumped into his throat. He glanced at his watch. He had another hour before Geneva would be home with the kids. He was supposed to be working from home, reviewing specs for new additions to his line of tools, but this felt like a much better use of his time.

He stepped out onto his back patio, taking Marigold with him, and answered the call.

"Hey," he said.

A beat of silence, a deep breath, and then he heard, "I miss you, too. So much."

Harry couldn't stop himself from smiling. Dared he even hope?

"Zoey, I'm so sorry I ever made you feel like you should walk away from your career for me. I was an idiot. I wasn't thinking about how it looked from your perspective because I was too focused on what I wanted, on how much I wanted to be with you."

"I know," Zoey said, her voice soft. "I get it."

"Please trust me when I say it won't ever be like that. If you want to have a career, I want you to have one. Here or there, or anywhere. If you ever decided you wanted to stay at home with our kids, I would support that too." He froze. He'd just said kids. *Our* kids. "Oh, man. Please erase that last sentence and pretend like you didn't hear me reference our future children."

Zoey laughed. "I like the sound of future children with you, Harrison Beckford."

"I'm so sorry, Zoey. Truly."

"I'm sorry, too. I shouldn't have left like I did. I should have been more transparent about the job I was trying to get and just, well, everything."

"How is the job?" Harry asked. "Do you like it?"

"Yes," she replied immediately. "I mean, no. I mean, yes, I love it, but not enough to keep doing it, I don't think. I'm not saying this the right way. I have so many things I want to say and I'm not . . . I can't stop thinking about ridiculous questions. Like about whether or not your new nanny is young and beautiful and whether or not you've been seeing anyone and whether or not you might consider seeing *me* again if I happened to come back to California."

Harry laughed. "Geneva is sixty-five. She's a lovely woman, but she's older than my mom, and she's been married for forty years. Don't get me wrong. I've tried. But so far, she's rejected all my invitations."

Zoey chuckled. "I've missed your teasing."

"I'm not seeing anyone, Zoey. How could I possibly think about dating anyone else when I'm still so in love with you?"

CHAPTER 21

ZOEY CLOSED HER EYES, pressing her phone against her chest for a brief moment before lifting it back to her ear.

An alarm buzzed on Zoey's phone. If she didn't leave for the station in the next five minutes, she'd be giving her producers a heart attack.

"I have to go to work," she said. "But can I call you later? Can we talk? Really talk?"

Harry hesitated before saying, "Of course. I'll be around. Call me as soon as you can."

Zoey ended the call knowing she'd left Harry hanging. He'd said I love you, and she'd said can I call you later?

But she couldn't say I love you over the phone. Not for the first time.

Her bosses were maybe going to hate her for this.

Possibly enough that she might lose her job.

She willed her mind to slow down long enough to make

some plans. She wasn't going to work today, but she couldn't leave them anchorless. She texted a quick message to Sarah, the morning news anchor she'd gotten to know over the past couple of months. Sarah responded almost immediately, agreeing to cover for her. Zoey sent *that* confirmation, along with a vague explanation of her absence to her bosses, hoping they'd forgive her since she'd found someone to fill her seat.

Then she headed for the hall closet to grab her suitcase.

She had a plane to catch.

CHAPTER 22

HARRY WAITED ALL AFTERNOON for Zoey to call. Then all evening.

Had he scared her away by admitting he still loved her? He hadn't planned to say it. But when she'd admitted to missing him, and then gotten jealous over his new nanny, it had just sort of tumbled out. He didn't regret saying it. But he maybe regretted saying it so soon.

Just after midnight, someone buzzed the outer gate at the end of his driveway.

He pulled out his phone, immediately recognizing Zoey's silhouette standing in the darkness outside the gate. He opened the gate remotely, watching through the feed long enough to make sure she got back in her Uber so the driver could bring her up the long driveway. She could have walked it, but as late it was, he would have hated for her to have to.

Excitement pulsed in Harry's chest as he padded to the entryway and swung open the front door. Zoey was already climbing out of the car. He waited where he stood, watching her, mesmerized by her. She was here. Close enough to touch. Close enough to kiss.

She pulled her suitcase toward him, stopping at the bottom of the porch stairs. She looked travel-worn and weary, but her eyes were bright, her smile stretching all the way across her face.

"I'm sorry I didn't call you back," she said as the Uber pulled away.

He ran a hand across his hair. "Yeah. You had me worried there for a little while."

She lifted her shoulders into a shrug. "I just couldn't stand the thought of saying I love you for the first time over the phone."

Harry was down the porch steps in a flash, scooping Zoey into his arms. He breathed her in, everything about the way her hair smelled to the way she fit in his arms feeling just so right. He tilted his head and pressed his lips against hers, his hands cradling her cheeks. Only then did he notice the tears sliding down her face.

"Hey, what's wrong? Are you okay?" he asked.

She sniffed and hiccupped out a laugh. "I'm okay. It's just been a really long afternoon. I couldn't get a flight at first, so I had to fly standby. When I finally did get on a flight, the plane had mechanical difficulties and was rerouted to Phoenix, so I had to get on a different flight, and this time I was sitting next to this very smelly older man who kept trying to talk to me about popcorn sales—he's an actual popcorn salesman—and through it all, the only way I managed to keep it together was to imagine over and over what this moment was going to be like." She sniffed again and wiped her eyes. "I mean, my imagination is pretty good." She leaned up and kissed him. "But not this good."

"Come on," Harry said, reaching for her suitcase. "Let's go inside."

There was so much he wanted to talk to her about. So much they *needed* to talk about. But Zoey looked exhausted. He led her to the couch where he sat down and opened his arms. She fell right into them, resting her head on his chest and wrapping her arms around his midsection. He pressed a kiss to her temple, fighting the urge to release the litany of questions he had building inside of him.

Had she quit her job? If she hadn't yet, was she going to? Was she okay about that? Was she moving back for good? Did she have a plan?

Zoey breathed in and out deeply, relaxing further into his arms. "I'm really happy, Harry," she whispered.

He smiled to himself. That wasn't the first time she'd said that to him. Had the first time been the night of the charity event they'd attended together? He couldn't quite remember. But it didn't matter. She was home. In his arms. And she loved him. What more could he ask for than that?

"Yeah," he whispered into her ear. "I'm really happy too."

The next morning, Zoey showed up in the kitchen while the

kids were still at the kitchen table eating their breakfast before school.

The guest room where she'd slept was far enough away from the main part of the house he'd hoped she'd sleep late, but when he saw Hannah's face as Zoey walked into the room, he was glad Zoey had decided to join them.

"Zoey?!" Hannah yelled. She jumped from her chair and raced around the island, colliding with Zoey's legs.

"Oof," Zoey said. "It's nice to see you too, Hannah." She moved around the table and ran her hand across Oliver's hair. "Hi, Ollie." She leaned down and kissed his cheek.

Oliver smiled and held up his spoon. "Oatmeal?" he asked, offering her a bite.

Zoey leaned in and took the bite, offering Harry a wide, slightly scared smile. "Hmmm," she said. "Thank you for sharing." Emotion swelled in Harry's chest. How had they ever survived without her?

"Are you going to stay this time?" Hannah asked. "Forever?"

Zoey looked up and caught Harry's eye. "I do have to go back to Chicago for a little bit, but it should only be for a few days. Then I'm moving back here for good."

A weight he hadn't realized was there suddenly lifted off of Harry's shoulders.

"Will you be our nanny again?" Hannah asked.

Out of the corner of his eye, Harry saw Geneva stiffen.

"No, baby," Zoey said. "In Chicago I worked for a news station on TV. When I move back, I'll have to find a news station here that I can work for. But I promise, we'll still be together lots, even if I'm not your nanny."

Hannah leaned back, looking up at Zoey's face with a contemplative expression so deep, Harry could see it from where he stood across the kitchen. Hannah motioned for Zoey to bend down, where she whispered something in her ear, after glancing back at her dad just briefly.

Zoey smiled at Hannah's words, whatever they were, catching Harry's gaze before looking back to Hannah. She whispered something back, and Hannah grinned, wide-eyed, before moving back to the table.

Harry moved across the kitchen, wrapping his arms around Zoey before tugging her around the corner into the living room. His kids might not care if he kissed Zoey good morning, but he still wasn't sure Geneva wouldn't scold him. "Good morning," he whispered. He kissed Zoey gently on the lips.

"Good morning."

"Are you really moving back for good?"

Zoey nodded. "I've already got a few calls in to producers in the area. I made good use of my layover yesterday. And I talked to *my* producers also, and they're going to see about reaching out to our affiliate networks to see if they can put in a good word for me."

Harry ran his hands up and down her arms. "That's really great news."

Zoey shrugged. "I shouldn't have been so afraid of the possibility."

Harry leaned down and kissed her one more time.

"What was that all about back there with Hannah? What did she whisper to you?"

Zoey grinned. "A lady never tells her secrets."

Harry groaned playfully. "Oh, don't make me play this game. You know if you don't tell me, I'll get it out of Hannah."

"You will not, Daddy," Hannah yelled from the kitchen. "I'll never tell."

"You're back in the house less than twelve hours, and already you're conspiring against me?"

"Absolutely," Zoey said. "We girls have to stick together."

After one more kiss, Zoey retreated to take a shower and Harry went back and joined the kids at the kitchen table. Hannah had already finished and was carrying her plate over to Geneva when he sat down. On her way back to the table, she wrapped her tiny arms around Harry's neck. "Don't tell Zoey I told," Hannah whispered, "but what I asked her is if she was going to be our mommy since she isn't our nanny anymore. And she said yes, as long as you ask her one day. Which is why I'm telling her secret, Daddy. So that one day, you can ask."

Harry reached up and patted his daughter's arms, hope filling his chest so full he thought he might burst. "One day, huh?" he asked. "You don't have an opinion about when?"

Hannah rolled her eyes. "Well, she just got here so maybe not today," she said with dramatic flair. "You should at least let her unpack her suitcase first. But maybe like, on Wednesday."

"Wednesday? I'll take that into consideration."

It *was* on a Wednesday that Harry proposed, though he waited a few more months to do it. He figured Zoey deserved the chance not just to unpack, but to get a job—which happened in a matter of days, not weeks; apparently Zoey was very good at what she did—and get settled into her new California life before he asked her to marry him.

When the perfect Wednesday arrived, Harry put on his favorite suit, dressed his kids in their fanciest clothes—Oliver had on suspenders and an orange bowtie—and declared that they were all skipping school, and work, so they could chase down their family.

Zoey had opted to move back in with her grandmother, both because she believed Emily still benefited from the company even if she didn't need the care, and, Harry hoped, because she anticipated a wedding in their future as much as he did. Neither of them had said as much out loud, not to anyone but Hannah, but they'd talked around the subject enough, he was pretty sure they were on the same page.

Harry hadn't come to see Zoey with much of a plan. He'd just woken up that morning, looked at the bright blue sky and decided it was a good Wednesday to get engaged. He only had an hour or two before Zoey would leave for work, though maybe after the proposal, he could convince her to play hooky with the rest of them.

Spring was in full bloom in Ms. Emily's backyard. Zoey had taken to doing morning yoga in the shade of the orange tree in the back of the lot. She was still there when Harry stepped through the back door, a kid holding onto each of his hands.

When Zoey looked up and saw them standing there, she smiled. "What is this?" she asked, walking toward them. "You all look so nice! What are we so dressed up for?" For a moment, she looked slightly panicked. "Did I forget something?"

Harry shook his head. "Nope. Nothing."

She narrowed her eyes. "Okay. Then, what's up?"

"I told Daddy he should wait for a Wednesday. And that's today," Hannah said, heavy emphasis on the today.

Harry swallowed and closed his eyes for a brief moment before steeling his nerves and stepping forward. He took Zoey's hand. "Zoey?"

"Yeah," she said, a tremble in her voice.

He dropped to one knee. "Marry me?" He looked over his shoulder at his kids. "Marry us?"

Zoey leaned forward, cradling Harry's face in her hands and kissed him softly. "Yes," she whispered. She looked at the kids, motioning them forward. "Yes," she said again. "Yes to all of you."

EPILOGUE

"HANNAH! WHERE ARE YOU?" Zoey called up the stairs. "Do you have Oliver with you?"

"We're coming!" Oliver called.

He showed up in the living room first, his hair mussed and sticking up in every direction. He held a pair of navy-blue shorts in his hands. "I found them," he said, holding them up. "Just where you said they'd be."

"Mommies just know these things, Oliver," Hannah said, entering the room. She already wore a pair of dark blue jeans, just like Zoey had asked.

"Do these work?" she asked.

"Yep. They're perfect. Here, Ollie. Let's get you into your shorts." She glanced at her watch. Location sharing on Google Maps told her Harry would be home in less than ten minutes. She suddenly wished for a surge of traffic to slow him down, just to give her a few extra minutes of prep time.

After an October wedding, she'd moved into Harry's house and taken on the official role of stepmom, though the kids had long since started calling her Mom. Hannah still called her Zoey occasionally, but Oliver had called her mommy right from the start. It hadn't always been smooth sailing; building a marriage while also adjusting to family life had its own unique set of challenges, but Zoey had the world's greatest partner.

And it's a good thing, because their life was about to get a lot more complicated.

Zoey pulled the shirts she'd ordered for just this occasion out of her bag. "Okay, guys. I've got to tell you something really big, okay? And you should feel really special because you're the first two people in the whole world that I've told."

Hannah's eyes went wide. "You haven't even told Daddy?"

Zoey shook her head. "Nope. But you're going to help me tell him today. Can you help me do that?"

They both nodded. Zoey held up Hannah's shirt, turned to face her so Hannah could read what it said.

"Big Sister," Hannah said. Her eyebrows scrunched up and her nose wrinkled. Underneath the "Big Sister," the word *Again* was written in parenthesis.

"This one's for you, Oliver," Zoey said. "It says *Big Brother.*"

"But I'm not a big brother, silly," Oliver said.

"Not yet," Zoey said. "But you're going to be. Next year, we're going to have another baby in the house."

Hannah gasped. "A baby? Really?"

Oliver smiled. "Can it be a boy?"

"No!" Hannah said, her hands on her hips. "It's going to be a girl like Auntie Charlotte's new baby."

Zoey laughed. "We don't get to pick, guys. It might be a girl or a boy. We just have to wait and see."

"So Daddy's going to come in and see our shirts?" Hannah said. "That's how we're telling him?"

"Yep," Zoey said. "Cute idea, right? I thought you could be standing together in the living room when he walks in."

"Or!" Hannah said, her finger sticking up like she had a great idea. It was one of Zoey's favorite Hannah-isms. "What if we put on the shirts, but then we don't say anything? We just do normal stuff like watching TV and making dinner like it's no big deal? We could see how long it takes him to notice."

Zoey actually liked the idea. "Okay, but if he hasn't noticed by the end of dinner, we're going to have to get a little obvious. Good plan?"

They nodded. "Good plan," Oliver said.

Zoey forced her hands into her back pockets when Harry kissed her hello. He narrowed his eyes at her, as if he could sense the energy buzzing around her, but he didn't say anything. He reached down and swung Oliver into his arms, blowing raspberries on his neck before putting him back onto the floor. Zoey tensed, waiting for him to notice, and Hannah giggled, but Harry still didn't say anything.

"It's a gorgeous day out," he said, walking toward the back door. "You guys want to take Marigold for a walk?"

"Um, what if we just hang out in the backyard for a little bit?"

she said. She loved being outside, but she wasn't exactly ready to advertise their news to anyone who happened upon them on the street. Talk about a way to grab headlines.

Harry gave her a funny look and she shrugged. "I'm just tired. Tough yoga class this morning."

"Okay. That's cool too. How was your day, Hannah?" he asked, rustling his hand over his daughter's hair.

"So good, Daddy," she said. "I'd love to play outside with you."

Zoey almost rolled her eyes. Hannah deserved an *A* plus for her acting, but she seemed anything but normal, her words over enunciated, her gestures too intentional.

Harry looked from Hannah, to Oliver, then back to Zoey. "What's going on with you guys? Am I missing something?"

Zoey only shrugged. "I have no idea what you're talking about."

Hannah mimicked her. "Me neither, Daddy. Everything is totally normal."

It was Oliver who finally cracked, collapsing into a fit of giggles. "It's our shirts, Daddy. Read our shirts!"

Hannah scoffed, her indignation real. "Oliver! You weren't supposed to tell him!"

Zoey reached a hand out for Hannah, shushing her, even as she watched Harry bend down and study Oliver's shirt. Without looking up, he motioned for Hannah to come closer, reading her shirt just as he had Ollie's. Zoey's heart pinged with happiness. Even while processing her very big news, Harry had made sure each of his kids got to be a part of the moment.

He pulled both kids to his chest without saying a word, then stood up, finally turning to face Zoey. He sniffed, wiping what looked suspiciously like tears from his eyes and crossed the kitchen to where she stood. "For real?" he asked, wrapping his arms around her waist.

She grinned. "For real."

He hugged her tightly. "And you're happy?"

She laughed. "So happy."

"Three kids?" he asked. "Can we handle three kids?"

She shrugged. "I'm not sure we're going to have much of a choice. But yes," Zoey said, leaning up to kiss her husband. "Together, I think we can handle anything."

Made in the USA
Middletown, DE
17 June 2025